IRISH STORIES

BY

JOHN B. KEANE

ROBERTS RINEHART PUBLISHERS

Boulder, Colorado

Published in the United States and Canada by Roberts Rinehart Publishers,
6309 Monarch Park Place, Niwot, Colorado 80503
Tel 303.652.2685 • Fax 303.652.2689

Visit our website at www.robertsrinehart.com

Distributed to the trade by Publishers Group West

First published in Ireland by Mercier Press

Text copyright © 1998 John B. Keane

Library of Congress Catalog Card Number 98–87576

ISBN 1-57098-070-5 [hardback]
ISBN 1-57098-242-2 [paperback]

10 9 8 7 6 5 4 3 2 1

Book design:
Ann W. Douden

Typesetting:
Red Barn Publishing, Skeagh, Skibbereen, Co. Cork, Ireland

Printed in the United States of America

CONTENTS

GLOSSARY

bohareen, boreen	narrow road
cadhrawns	bits and pieces
deoch an dorais	a drink for the road
gabhail	an armful
poitcheen	illegal homemade whiskey
puck	kick
reek	heap of turf neatly clamped
skeeved	skimmed
sláinte	your health, cheers
slean	turf-spade
sliotar	hurling ball
spailpín	wandering laborer
stooking	stacking
stoolin	heap of dried turf (peat)
sugawn	straw-woven chair
taspy	energy, eagerness
turtóg	small mound
ullagones	wails

Fred Rimble

Fred Rimble was born in Maggie Conlon's bedroom in Dirreenroe at three minutes past seven on the evening of September 7, 1979. The event was not marked by any unusual celestial manifestations nor was there the least furore in the more immediate circumjacence of Dirreenroe.

"Indeed," said Maggie Conlon's son Jim at a later date, "I would not have brought the poor creature into the world at all but for being driven to it by my mother's ear-ache."

At seventy-five Maggie Conlon belied her age by several years. Her hair still retained most of its natural black. Her eyes were bright and clear. Her step was free of infirmity and, while she would never admit to it, the hearty appetite which she had enjoyed all her life still remained with her, completely unimpaired.

She should, therefore, have been fairly well pleased with the general state of her health and, of course, if you were also to take into account the fact that she was relatively well-to-do you should not be blamed for believing that her all-round lot was a happy one.

Alas the opposite was the case. Maggie Conlon was a hypochondriac. Local doctors could find nothing the matter with her but hope springs eternal so Maggie fared as far afield as her means would allow and consulted unsuccessfully with several noted specialists. She then resorted to quacks after the fashion of all true hypochondriacs and, despite temporary cures of the most dramatic nature, continued to provide local doctors and pharmacists with a solid source of income.

The mystery was that she managed to survive the vast and varied intake of potions and pills not to mention the liniments and lotions with which she harassed the countless aches and skin diseases to which her hypersensitive exterior seemed always to be prey. The most malignant aspect of this particular type of hypochondria was, while it failed to hasten the demise of Maggie Conlon, it had dispatched her two husbands to early graves.

Both had been hard-working men who needed rest and

care after their day's labors. Neither, unfortunately, was forthcoming from Maggie. From dawn till dark both husbands were on call. Poultices were constantly in demand as were hot drinks, gargles and numerous other medicaments. These necessitated regular journeys upstairs and downstairs all through the night. Fine if Maggie was available in the morning to cook a sustaining breakfast and provide a nourishing lunch pack or if she was on her feet in the evening with a warm welcome and a warmer meal. Instead she was confined to bed and during those rare intervals when no pain troubled her she went around with her head and face muffled, with her body totally covered and smelling all the time of powerful prophylactics.

Whether or not she succeeded in warding off occupational diseases and wayward drafts was anybody's guess but one thing was certain. The germs of romance which might have blossomed in perfumed surrounds into rich and rewarding love were slowly but surely exterminated by the deadly disinfectants in which her garments abounded. The marriages had started out well enough. In the beginning there had been affection, a close relationship in both cases which might have been nurtured into something more rewarding if Maggie had shown the least desire to relinquish her unnatural preoccupation with her health.

Jim Conlon was the sole outcome of the marriages, presenting himself to the world shortly after the demise of his father, Maggie's second husband. At the time an unkind neighbor was heard to say that the poor man had precipitated his own death with the awful prospect that the issue might be female and that he would be faced with two Maggies instead of one. The truth was he died of fatigue. Maggie Conlon had worn him out just as she had worn out his predecessor. There are some men who thrive off selfish wives, who excel themselves as husbands in the face of such adversity. There are others who suffer in silence, waiting for death to rescue them. Maggie's pair were of this latter mold.

Her son Jim was a mild-mannered, easy-going fellow who asked little of the world. His job, a bookkeeper in the local creamery, was undemanding. His wages were more than adequate. He lived with his mother. He might have married but progress in that direction was brought to an immediate halt as soon as any likely contender encountered Maggie.

One particular girl with whom he had made considerable headway spelled out her terms unequivocally after a visit to Maggie.

"I'm willing to marry you," she told Jim, "and I'm willing to devote the rest of my life to you but it will have to be in a town or city a long way from here."

"I just can't walk out on her altogether," he pleaded. "After all she is my mother."

"I'm not asking you to walk out on her," the girl explained. "You can visit her from time to time and she can visit us if she feels like it. You have your own life to live and I'm sure your mother will accept this when you explain it to her."

"I never heard the like," Maggie Conlon had retorted

bitterly when Jim had laid his cards on the table. "I mean it's not as if I were asking the pair of you to come and live with me under this roof and anyway where are you going to get another job if you leave Dirreenroe? Have you thought of that?"

"Oh, I'll get another job all right," Jim assured her. "With my experience that should be no trouble."

The following afternoon Maggie Conlon lay in a hospital bed as a result of an inexplicable collapse on her way from the butcher's earlier that morning. The doctors were mystified. Her heart was strong, her pulse steady, her blood pressure normal. She was released after a week with a clean bill of health after Jim had declared that he would never leave Dirreenroe.

Now at thirty-one he began, at last, to see the writing on the wall. The constant complaining had begun to take its toll. At work he wondered what new malaise would be awaiting him when he arrived home. It was not till he found himself on the threshold of mental disintegration that he brought Fred Rimble into the world. That morning before he left for work his mother had complained of a severe backache. Jim had called the family doctor but that worthy could find nothing wrong. When Jim arrived home for lunch his mother was still in bed. The ache in the back had removed itself and was now resident in the neck. When he finally finished work he was surprised to hear it had ended up in the left ear after a horrendous journey from its original starting place.

"I won't get a wink of sleep tonight," she complained

when he suggested she abandon the bed and share the stew which he had prepared for both of them. He pleaded in vain.

"I couldn't look at a bite," she said which meant that she had eaten while he was at work. After he had washed and stowed the ware he returned to the bedroom. Her martyred face was barely visible through an opening in the red flannelette with which she had bound her head. The bed clothes were drawn tightly under her chin. Every so often a distraught moan punctuated her affected wheezing.

"No one has an ear like mine," she whined.

"I don't know," Jim spoke casually. "A chap had his ear chopped off at the creamery today, his left ear."

Maggie Conlon raised herself painfully on her elbows.

"Had his left ear chopped off?"

"His left ear," Jim confirmed.

"Was he from Dirreenroe?" Maggie removed the red flannelette the better to catch the answer.

"From Dublin," Jim confirmed.

"Oh the poor man." Maggie was all concern. "What hospital did they take him to?"

"No hospital," Jim told her.

"But I don't understand. You say he had his ear chopped off."

"Yes. He had his left ear chopped off."

"And he didn't go to hospital?"

"As far as I know."

Maggie sat upright in the bed. "I'm afraid I don't understand."

Jim rose from the side of the bed where he had seated himself. He sighed and went to the window. His gaze swept the evening sky before he spoke.

"He was demonstrating an electric potato peeler," he explained slowly, "and the next thing you know the damn thing stopped. He bent down right where the potato goes in and off she starts without warning."

"And the ear?"

"He put it in a bucket of ice and clapped a handkerchief over the wound and then hit for Dublin to have it sewn back on."

"What did you say his name was?" Maggie Conlon asked.

"Fred Rimble," Jim replied.

"I don't know any Rimbles," Maggie said.

"How could you when he doesn't come from around here. I told you he came from Dublin."

When he arrived home for lunch the following day he found his mother up and about. The pain in the ear had partially disappeared and for a change a hot meal awaited him.

"Any news of Fred Rimble?" Maggie asked.

Jim was taken unawares but he took advantage of a mouthful of mashed potatoes to hide his surprise. As he masticated needlessly his imagination worked overtime. Finally he spoke.

"He's lucky to be alive is Fred Rimble."

"Did he get back to Dublin?"

"Not off his own bat. He fainted in the car from loss of

blood and crashed into a telephone pole."

"Oh, my God!" Maggie Conlon cried. "What happened then?"

"He was taken by ambulance to Dublin. Apparently the ice spilled from the bucket with the impact of the crash. The ear was thrown onto the roadway and could not be found. They fear a magpie may have made off with it or a gray crow or the likes."

As his mother made the Sign of the Cross he hurriedly re-addressed himself to his meal. He realized her interest was thoroughly aroused. Bent over his plate, he prepared himself for her next question.

"Is he married?"

"Yes."

"Has he a family?"

"Eight. Four boys and four girls."

"May God protect them," Maggie Conlon whispered and she made the Sign of the Cross a second time.

Jim left for work earlier than usual. He needed time to think out a plan of campaign. He wondered how long he could continue with the deception. For the present he would do no more than release minor bulletins concerning the loss of the ear and the effects of same on Fred Rimble. Every weekend Jim Conlon spent most of his time in a neighborhood tavern. He liked a few drinks and there was the added bonus of a reprieve from the pathological out-pourings of his mother. It was here he thought up the idea of providing Fred with a plastic ear.

"You're very thoughtful lately, Jim boy," Matt Weir the

publican interrupted his conceptions.

"Friend of mine," Jim explained, "took a bad turn lately."

"Sorry to hear that, Jim boy." Matt Weir patted him on the shoulder and moved off to comfort any other lone birds who might be on the premises.

A week after the accident, Maggie took to the bed again. She blamed an old ankle injury which had been aggravated by a sudden change in the weather. Again Jim found himself fending for both of them. Maggie spent three full days in bed and might have spent three weeks had not Jim resorted to his friend Fred Rimble. When he returned for lunch on the third day he found her with the clothes tucked up to her chin. Her head was almost completely muffled by the red flannelette. The martyred look had returned to her face. The room reeked of recently-applied embrocation and every so often there were the old familiar sighs of untold suffering.

"This will be the death of me," Maggie said.

Jim sat silently on the bed and carefully prepared his release.

"God alone knows what I go through," Maggie groaned.

"Fred Rimble's wife left him."

The announcement was made matter of factly. It took some time before Maggie was able to transfer from herself to this latest development.

"Was there another man?" she asked after a while.

"Afraid so," Jim said.

"A neighbor I'll warrant."

"Right first time," Jim confirmed. "His best friend to boot."

Wisely Jim arose and left the room. Maggie's next question might prove too much for him. She was on her feet early the following morning. A fine breakfast awaited him when he came downstairs. While he dined, Maggie spoke of the perfidy of neighbors. She roundly cursed the ruffian who stole Fred Rimble's wife.

Weeks were to pass before she took ill again, this time with nothing more than a crick in the neck. Maggie's cricks, however, were like no other. They might last for weeks or develop into far more sinister aches. Jim roused her by the simple expedient of telling her that Fred Rimble had broken both legs in another car crash. By the time the New Year was due, Fred Rimble had, in addition to his earlier mishaps, broken his collar bone, both hands, numerous ribs and to crown his misfortune lost his second ear. It was the removal of the remaining auricle which provided Jim with the happiest Christmas he had spent since childhood. Maggie went around all through the festive period shaking her head and bemoaning the terrible loss. Her Christmas was, however, pain-free.

When he informed her about the second ear, Maggie suggested that he contact Fred and invite him and the children to spend Christmas with them.

"No," Jim had answered sagely. "I know Fred. He's the sort of man who would want to spend Christmas at home."

"But who's going to cook the Christmas dinner?"

"No problem there," Jim informed her. "The eldest girl is fifteen and then there's a woman nearby who looks in now and then."

"What woman nearby?" Maggie asked suspiciously.

"Just a neighbor," Jim replied.

Maggie searched his face to see if he was concealing anything. "She wouldn't be by any chance the missus of the man who went off with Fred's wife?"

"No chance," Jim assured her. "Fred isn't that sort."

"Of course not," Maggie responded at once, "that was not what I meant."

Spring came round before she complained again. Normally she would have spent the greater part of January in bed and the remainder muffled up downstairs. Every week or ten days, Jim would dole out what he privately termed a Rimble ration. Maggie awaited the tidbits eagerly and gobbled up each and every one with relish. In January, Jim was obliged to dispose by drowning of the eldest daughter whose name was Cornelia and of the youngest who answered to the name of Trixie. He had good reason for resorting to such extremes. His mother had taken suddenly to the bed one wet afternoon on the grounds that she had undergone a serious heart attack. Even the family doctor who knew her every gambit was perplexed.

"It is just possible," he confided to Jim, "that she may have suffered the mildest of coronaries."

Jim sensed that a broken limb would not be sufficient this time nor indeed the loss of a hand or a leg. Her appetite had been whetted. She now needed stronger meat if a cure was to be effected. For this reason he felt obliged to dispose of Cornelia and Trixie. Maggie had jumped out of bed upon hearing the news, her heart miraculously cured.

"That's one funeral I'm not going to miss," she announced. Try as he might Jim could not dissuade her. The following morning, she rose early and purchased a daily paper. Painstakingly, she went through the death notices.

"Rattigan, Remney, Reeves," she intoned the names solemnly. "Riley, Romney, Rutledge. There's no Rimble here."

"I know Fred Rimble," Jim said. "Fred hates any sort of a show. The funeral would, of course, be private. That's why it's not in the papers."

"We'll send him a telegram then," Maggie insisted, "and a letter of sympathy. I'll write it myself."

"Of course," Jim agreed. "I'll send the telegram this very morning. You go ahead and write your letter and I'll post it for you during the lunch break."

At his office in the creamery Jim burned the letter. A week later, he typed a reply using a fictitious Dublin address. The letter proved the best tonic Maggie ever received. It kept her out of bed for several weeks. When its effects wore off, he did away with the other children pair by pair, the first by food poisoning, the second by a car accident and the third by fire. Indeed Fred Rimble himself had been lucky to escape the conflagration with his life. The last proved to be a wise choice. Since the family home had been razed to the ground Fred was left without a permanent address.

The deaths of the Rimble children had a profound effect on Maggie. She took to attending early mass on a regular basis. Regardless of the weather she never once opted out. She enquired daily after Fred but news was scant. He had, it was reported, left the country and taken up work in Australia.

"Too many memories in the home place," Maggie had observed when Jim informed her of Fred's departure. "I imagine that if it were me I would do the very same thing," she said wistfully.

Summer passed. Autumn russetted the leaves and the winds laid them out lovingly on the soft earth. Jim Conlon grew fat and content.

"There's a shine to you lately, Jim boy," Matt Weir told him one night.

Then winter came and inevitably Maggie Conlon took to the bed. In spite of assurances from her own doctor and from a specialist she became convinced that she was suffering from cancer of the throat. She submitted herself to X-rays and to countless other tests. The net result was that there was no evidence whatsoever to show that there was the least trace of the dread disease of which she complained. The weeks passed and when no decline set in she became even more insistent that cancer had taken hold of her windpipe. To prove it she fell back upon a comprehensive repertoire of wheezes, many of them spine-chilling, others weak and pathetic.

The contentment to which Jim Conlon had grown accustomed became a thing of the past. He lost weight. All the old tensions with some new ones in their wake returned to bedevil him. He tried every ruse to rouse his mother but all to no avail. She became so morbid in herself that she made him go for the parish priest every week. When the last rites were administered she would close her eyes as if resigning herself to death. In the end, Jim was driven to his wit's end. One night he returned from the pub in what seemed to be a highly agitated state. In reality, he was playing the last trump left in his hand.

"I've just had some dreadful news," he informed his mother.

The lackluster eyes showed no change nor did she adjust her position in the bed.

"Fred Rimble is dead," Jim told her.

The news had the desired effect. At once she sat upright.

"How did it happen?" she asked after she had crossed herself and begged God's mercy on his soul.

"They say he died of a broken heart," Jim informed her.

"A broken heart!" she exclaimed tearfully and wondered why she had never thought of this novel way out herself.

"That's what they said," Jim spoke with appropriate sadness.

"Well, it's all behind him now, the poor man," Maggie Conlon spoke resignedly. A few days later at Maggie's insistence they had a High Mass said for Fred Rimble in

Dirreenroe parish church. It was an unpretentious affair with no more than the three priests, the parish clerk and themselves involved. As soon as they arrived home, Maggie prepared lunch and, when they had eaten, she went at once to her bed, vowing that she would never leave it.

"But what's wrong with you?" Jim asked in anguish. "You were fine ten minutes ago. You put away a feed fit for a ploughman."

"I know. I know," she said weakly, "but the bitter truth is that I think my heart is beginning to break."

"This beats all," Jim fumed.

"Now, now," said Maggie. "You mustn't let it upset you. It's not in the least like a coronary or angina. There's nothing like the pain. I'll just lie here now and wait for my time to come."

She closed her eyes and a blissful look settled on her face.

In the tavern, Jim sat on his own in a deserted corner. Midway through his third drink, Matt Weir came from behind the counter and saluted him. When he didn't answer, Matt asked if there was anything wrong.

"Look at me, Matt," Jim spoke despondently. "Look at me and tell me what you see."

"I see a friend and a neighbor," Matt Weir answered.

"No, Matt," Jim countered. "What you see is a man who killed the best friend he ever had."

Faith

The brothers Fly-Low lived in an ancient farmhouse astride a bare hillock which dominated their rushy fields. Tom Fly-Low was the oldest of the three. Next in age came Billy and lastly there was Jack.

Fly-Low, of course, was a sobriquet. The surname proper was Counihan. It was never used except by the parish priest once every five years when he read the Station lists.

In the year 1940 an Irish reconnaissance plane flew over the Fly-Low farm. At the time, the brothers were in the meadow turning hay. As soon as the plane appeared, they stopped work and, lifting their hayforks aloft, welcomed the unique intrusion. Acknowledging the salute, the pilot dipped his wings.

"Fly low," Jack Counihan called.

"Fly low," shouted his brothers. "Fly low, fly low," they all called together. Alas, the pilot was unable to hear them. In a few moments, the plane had disappeared from view, never again to be seen by the brothers Fly-Low. In neighboring fields, other haymakers heard the din. It was only a matter of time before the Counihans would become known as the Fly-Lows. It was no more than the custom of the countryside. It made for easy identification, there being several other Counihan families in the nearby townlands.

Years later, at the end of the Second World War, there came one of the worst winters in living memory. When it wasn't awash with drenching rain, the winds blew searingly and searchingly. There were times when it froze and times when it thawed, times too when it snowed till the hills turned white. In between there was sleet, that awful conglomeration which can never make up its mind whether it's rain, snow or good round hailstone. There had been ominous signs from October onwards. Gigantic geese barbs imprinted the skies from an early stage. The bigger the skeins the blacker the outlook or so the old people said. On blackthorn and white were superabundances of sloe and haw, sure auguries of stormy days ahead. All the time the moon, full and otherwise, was never without a shroud. Then came an awesome night in the middle of

January. Before darkness fell, cautionary ramparts of puce-colored, impenetrable cloud were seen to make dusty inroads into an ever-changing sky. The wind blew loudly and, as night wore on, it blew louder still.

At midnight, a storm of unprecedented savagery ravaged the countryside. Wynds of hay were carried aloft and deposited in alien fields miles away. Trees were flattened and suspect haysheds gutted but, of all the destructive acts perpetrated that night, none was so capricious as that which swept the slates from the roof of Tom Fly-Low's bedroom. The rest of the house was left untouched. At half past one in the morning, the oldest of the Fly-Low brothers found himself staring upwards into a swirling sky.

Wise man that he was, he decided to stay abed till the storm spent itself. This it did as dawn broke mercifully over a devastated landscape.

After breakfast, the brothers inspected the damage. Structurally there was nothing the matter. They came to the conclusion that a sufficiency of second-hand slates was all that was required to repair the roof. They knelt beside the kitchen fire and offered a Rosary in thanksgiving. Immediately afterwards, the youngest brother Jack was commissioned to undertake the journey to the distant town of Listowel, there to forage among the premises of builders' providers for the necessary materials. Tom Fly-Low who acted as treasurer to the household counted fifty pounds in single notes into Jack's hands while Billy went in search of the black mare. She would be tackled to the brothers' only transport, a large common cart with iron-banded wheels.

Jack shaved in the kitchen and changed into his Sunday clothes. He dipped a brace of calloused fingers in the holy water font which hung just inside the front door, made the Sign of the Cross and went out of doors to begin the eleven-mile journey to the town. He was met in the cobbled yard by a fuming Billy. The mare had broken from the stable during the storm and was nowhere to be found. There was nothing for it but to walk to town and hope for a lift.

After the second mile, Jack stopped and lit his pipe. He sat in the lee of a densely-ivied hedge and allowed himself a brief rest. Around him the light green of well-grazed fields mottled with dung-induced clumps of richer grass shone in the winter sunlight. Birds sang in roadside bushes. Wearily he got to his feet and continued on his journey. As he did, an ancient Bedford truck appeared around a bend at his rear. Before he had time to hail it the driver had changed gears and brought it to a halt. Jack Fly-Low climbed into the cab.

The driver was a thin-faced, refined-looking man wearing a tattered black tam and faded overalls. After Jack had thanked him, there was silence for a mile or so.

"Don't I know you?" the driver asked.

"I don't see how you could," Jack told him. "I don't know you."

"My name is Florrie Feery," the driver introduced himself.

"And my name is Jack Counihan," Jack responded.

Half an hour passed without another word. At last they

found themselves in the suburbs of Listowel.

"Where here do you want to be dropped off?" Florrie asked.

Jack Fly-Low mentioned the name of a prominent builders' provider, "but," said he, "first I must stand you a drink."

The first drink borrowed a second and a third at which stage they had taken possession of two seats near a small table in a cosy corner of the bar. A turf fire burned brightly in a fireplace nearby. When Florrie rose to order a fourth drink, Jack protested. His business was pressing, he explained. There was no time to spare.

"What can be so pressing?" Florrie asked, "that won't keep till we've had a deoch an dorais?"

Instantly Jack felt ashamed. Here was this exceptional fellow who had picked him off the road when he might have been no more than a tramp or a common highwayman, who had asked for no reference when he opened the door of his cab, who only wanted to buy his round like any decent man. Over the fourth drink the conversation turned inwards on their personal business and respective families. Confidences were exchanged, as a result of which Jack Fly-Low decided to divulge his reason for being in town. Florrie listened sympathetically and attentively.

"That's a coincidence," he said half to himself, half to Jack, as soon as the latter had finished telling him about the disappearance of the slates.

"What is?" Jack asked.

"This chap near me back at home."

"What about him?"

"Nothing . . . except that he has an old house destined for demolition."

"And?"

"And," Florrie paused to sip his whiskey, "on the top of his house is the finest roof of second-hand slates you or me is ever like to see."

"It was God made our paths cross this morning," Jack Fly-Low said solemnly. "Do you think your man might be induced to sell the slates off this roof?"

Florrie permitted himself a deep chuckle. "Only this morning he asked me if I would be on the look-out for a buyer."

Thereafter they spoke in whispers at Florrie's insistence. There was the danger, he pointed out, that every Tom, Dick and Harry would get wind of the slates before he had time to close the deal on Jack's behalf. Caution, therefore, was of the essence. Because of his regard for Jack he would lay strong claim to a family relationship which existed between himself and the gentleman who owned the derelict house. He was of the opinion he could purchase and deliver the slates for a mere thirty pounds. Like a flash Jack Fly-Low's right hand went for his inside pocket. Florrie laid a restraining hand on his shoulder.

"Not here," he said, "let's go in the back."

In the makeshift toilet at the rear of the premises, the thirty pounds changed hands. A gentleman to the last, Florrie insisted in handing back a pound in luck money. There were more drinks before the truck driver recalled that he had promised to purchase a load of turf in a distant townland. There was an emotional goodbye and a promise that the slates would be delivered not later than noon of the following Saturday.

It was close to midnight when Jack Fly-Low arrived home. Billy and Tom were waiting by the hearth for an account of the day's activities. They listened spellbound as the youngest brother recounted the details of the day's outing. They were particularly impressed with his account of Florrie. Jack regaled them with different facets of the man's character until well into the morning. Whenever he flagged he would be prodded or prompted by Tom or Billy. They longed for Saturday so that they might see this paragon for themselves.

Early on Saturday a tradesman arrived to ready the roof for the slating. By noon he was in a position to start work in earnest but as the day wore on there was no sign of Florrie.

"He'll come," Jack told the others, "just give him time."

Every hour or so a mechanically propelled vehicle could be heard passing on the public road which passed by the extreme boundaries of the farm.

"Hush," Jack would call, "that's him now. That's him surely." The faces of the three brothers would light up expectantly whenever the noise of an engine was borne upward by the breeze. The tradesman smiled slyly to himself. There was the making of a good story here he told himself, a tale that would bear telling in the pub that night. At five o'clock he departed. He promised to return the moment the slates arrived.

The days passed but there was no sign of Florrie. Weeks went by, then months. Daffodils arrived to brighten the spring fields. The thorn buds quickened in the hedgerows but of Florrie and the slates there was no sign.

From time to time the tradesman would call to enquire if the materials had arrived. He volunteered to cover the roof temporarily with corrugated iron but the brothers would not hear of this. What would Florrie think? They had convinced themselves that he had been taken ill or that he had been involved in a serious accident.

The brothers Fly-Low had implicit trust in Florrie. Had not Jack spent a day with him, vetted him from all angles so to speak and convinced himself that he was an uncommonly fine fellow. Summer came and went and Tom's room still lay exposed to the elements. He moved to a settle bed in the kitchen. The brothers were agreed that it would be a breach of faith if they made any attempt to cover the roof before Florrie arrived. Arrive he would. Of that they were certain.

Whenever neighbors called to pass the time of day, one or other of the Fly-Lows would interrupt the conversation if the noise of traffic came from the roadway.

"Hush, hush," they would caution, "that could be Florrie with the slates."

It never was. In the houses around the neighboring countryside the whole business of the slates became something of a standing joke. Whenever a vehicle was heard passing, some member of the household was sure to say:

"Hush, hush now. That's Florrie with the slates."

For years it was a catch cry with younger folk ever on the alert for any form of diversion. It was without malice. No one would intentionally make fun of the Fly-Lows. They were good neighbors, deeply religious and charitable to a fault.

As the years rolled on mention of Florrie became rarer and rarer in the Fly-Low kitchen. At night when the boozing of a lorry was heard in the chimney the brothers would exchange hopeful looks but no word would pass between them. Of the three, Jack felt the disappointment most keenly. The others had not known Florrie like he had. Occasionally they might be forced to suppress nagging doubts and suspicions but having known the man in question he was never so affected.

The way Jack saw it any number of things could have happened. He recalled that Florrie was liberal with his money. This would not have escaped the notice of the numerous bar denizens who prey upon decenter types. Perhaps by now his body lay decomposed in some bog-hole or dyke. It was more likely, however, that an accident was responsible for his non-appearance. He had taken more than his fair share of drink on that memorable occasion in Listowel. For all Jack Fly-Low knew, the poor fellow could be dead and buried long since or maybe it was how he lost his memory. He had heard of cases where the memory failed altogether after excessive consumption of doubtful whiskey.

Anything was possible. Inevitably, Tom and Billy

decided the roof should be covered. Otherwise the entire house would suffer. As a concession, slates were not used. Instead, sheets of corrugated iron were hammered into place by the tradesman. The new roof was laid on in the spring. In the winter of that year, Tom Fly-Low passed away, having succumbed to a bout of pneumonia. His brothers were convinced that the corrugated-iron roof was responsible. They gave the room a wide berth after Tom's burial.

Then one windy night in the spring of the following year the distinct boozing of an oncoming lorry was heard in the chimney. From the increasing volume of the sound it was clear that it was heading for the house of the Fly-Lows. Jack and Billy rose together, their faces taut, not daring to breathe. His heart pounding, Jack opened the front door. Outside was a lorry. A man was alighting from the cab. He was approaching the doorway.

"Is it Florrie?" the barely whispered question came from Billy who stood at his brother's shoulder. The driver came nearer. Jack Fly-Low stood unmoving. Beside him Billy trembled uncontrollably. The driver was speaking: "Is this Dinnegan's?"

"No," Jack answered. "Go back the way you came. Dinnegan's is the next turn on the right."

The driver was squat, coarse and throaty. Florrie had been slender and tall, elegant almost. The driver re-entered his cab, reversed and drove off.

In the kitchen, Billy Fly-Low slumped against the table. The excitement had been too much for him. Unable to support himself, he fell to the floor. A strange, unearthly sound came from his throat. Jack knelt and whispered an act of contrition into his brother's ear.

Some months after the funeral a group of neighbors came to visit Jack Fly-Low. During the interval between the visit and the burial of Billy he had grown gaunt and feeble. The neighbors were concerned. It might be best if he sold the farm and moved to town where help would be at hand should any sudden misfortune befall him. No. He would never leave the old homestead. A housekeeper then? No. Why not let the farm? No. Jack Fly-Low was adamant. He would look after himself to the end. In spite of this the neighbors made an agreement between themselves that they would call regularly to see him.

The following December there came an unexpectedly heavy snow storm. A number of outlying houses were cut off for several days. Among these was the Fly-Low abode. As soon as the byroads were passable a neighbor made his way to the hillock. He found Jack in a sorry state. His breathing came irregularly and weakly. Often for long spells he would gasp for breath. The neighbor left hurriedly and found somebody to notify the priest and doctor. Quickly he returned and sat on the bedside holding Jack Fly-Low's hand while the numbered breaths grew fainter. The neighbor was relieved when at last he heard the sound of the priest's car in the driveway. Vainly Jack Fly-Low endeavored to raise himself to a sitting position. His throat crackled but no words came. His lips moved but no sound issued forth.

"What is it, Jack? What's the matter?" the neighbor asked anxiously.

Gathering the last vestiges of his vanishing strength, Jack Fly-Low opened his mouth. "Florrie," he whispered triumphantly before falling back on his pillow. His body slackened, the lips sealed themselves again but now there was the semblance of a smile on the shrunken dead face.

Guaranteed Pure

Willie Ramley came to Ireland for one purpose, to marry a virgin. In a New York tavern he had been informed by a man with a brogue as thick as a turnip that Ireland abounded in colleens of this caliber.

"How will I know she's a virgin?" Willie Ramley asked.

"You'll know," the man with the brogue assured him.

"But how?" Willie Ramley persisted.

"Take my word for it," the man with the brogue had said, "when the time comes all will be revealed." This had been the gist of the impartation.

Willie was halfway through his second month in Ireland and contrary to his expectations nothing whatever had been revealed. He had traveled far and wide but none of the girls he had encountered had appealed to him. The only one he had questioned regarding her virginity tagged him straight off with a right cross which would have done justice to a Golden Gloves middleweight. He ruefully pondered the advice tendered by the man with the brogue.

"All will be revealed," he had said. It had been late on Saint Patrick's night. The man with the brogue whose name he had forgotten was regarded as something of a seer by the other patrons of the tavern. They treated him with deference and placed double whiskies in front of him from time to time for no apparent reason other than to bask in his favor. Willie could not remember how the conversation had started. All he recalled was that he had babbled out the story of his life concluding with the latest and most tragic chapter which contained the sordid details of how his latest girlfriend had been two-timing him. The seer had placed a hand on his shoulder and looked him straight between the eyes. With the other hand he handed him an untouched glass of whiskey.

"Drink that," he had said, "and take note of what I tell you."

Willie Ramley did as he was bade.

"You see before you," said the seer, "a man who was once in the same quandary as yourself. My face is wrinkled now and my hair is gray but I was a sparkling fellow once, eager for love and living. These same gray hairs and wrinkles have been acquired at immense expense. They, therefore, give me the right to advise a young chap like yourself, not to pontificate, mark you, but to advise." Wiping a tear from his eye he handed Willie Ramley a second glass of whiskey.

"Wait," Willie had said, "let me buy you one."

"No," the seer had countered. "All those who come bearing me drinks have availed of my sagacity at one time or another. Should you and I meet again and should my counsel have proved to be beneficial I will expect a whiskey or two by way of compensation but for the present please regard these drinks which you see before me as much yours as mine."

Willie nodded in agreement, not wishing to interrupt with facile thanks the verbal flow of this most gracious old gentleman.

"When I was your age," the sage continued, "I jumped into matrimony with the first good-looking girl I saw. As a consequence the union was a disaster. It lasted three weeks. I was married secondly within six months and when that failed after a shorter period I vowed never again to marry. Oh vain resolve. In no time at all I was married again. You see, my dear boy, I was a martyr to matrimony. Seven times in all, I ventured into the matrimonial stakes and seven times I came a cropper."

At this juncture, Willie Ramley felt constrained to put in a short spake.

"I would marry only once," he said.

The seer was about to utter a caustic comment but

something in the young man's demeanor stayed him.

"I know how you feel," he said, "but marrying only once might not be so simple."

"I realize that," Willie told him, "but I am determined to succeed."

"Then," said the sage placing his hand upon the young man's shoulder for the second time, "you must be doubly careful."

"Counsel me please," Willie begged him. "Counsel me, I beseech you, before the years catch up with me and I am left to languish alone."

"This is what you must do," the seer said with a solemnity which became the problem. "You must betake yourself to Ireland from which sainted spot my mother, God rest her, emigrated to these less virtuous climes. She was truly an angel if ever there was one outside the sacred precincts of Heaven." Here the seer paused to acknowledge receipt of a wholesome shot of whiskey from a grateful client.

"Because you are pure yourself," the sage continued after he had sipped from the fresh bumper, "you seek a creature of equal purity."

Willie Ramley nodded eagerly. All his instincts firmly intimated that he had stumbled at last upon an authentic oracle.

"Do not," said the sage, "let yourself be carried away by the first pretty face nor by some coy damsel who will seem to be the answer to all your dreams. Be patient and the right girl will show herself. There will be something about her, something special that will set her apart from all others. This particular something will be as much in evidence as the nose on your very own face. It will be as clear as though it were stamped upon her back. Go now and keep your wits about you. Be continent in your ways and true to your ideal and she will make herself known to you in the manner in which I have indicated."

So saying, the sage lifted both hands in an elaborate flourish, indicating that he had said all he was going to say. Willie Ramley departed the scene and for weeks was fully absorbed by all that he had been told. He finally resolved that there was nothing for it but to travel to Ireland and it was thus that he found himself after six weeks, as far from attaining to his aspiration as he had been when he first set foot on the green land of Erin. Now, with less than a fortnight's time remaining to him he began to grow anxious and despaired of ever achieving his goal. So we find him in this despondent mood seated on a turtóg of snipegrass overlooking the vast beach of Ballybunion on a bright afternoon in the month of June.

Overhead, seagulls mewed in the scented seaside air whilst, around, the human race disported itself as though fine days were at a premium. Elders paddled in the shallow shorewater whilst young men ventured beyond their depth endeavoring to test the concern of those inshore females for whom they had a special eye. Toddlers toddled back and forth to the tide. Small boys and girls breathlessly shaped castles of sand with shovel and bucket whilst a golden-skinned lifeguard lorded it over all who sported in his domain. In short, it could be said that everybody was happy except Willie Ramley.

Tired of sitting in one place, he decided to venture uptown with a view to imbibing a cool drink in one of the resort's many excellent hostelries. As he dandered along, idly kicking empty cigarette and matchboxes with newly-purchased sandals, he was almost run down by a bus. Had it not been for the fact that a passer-by hollered an alarm, he might well have been injured. He managed to catch the barest glimpse of his benefactress, a shy young female who immediately averted her not unpretty head the moment she found his gaze turned in her direction. For a moment he stood unresolved outside the door of a popular tavern. The words of the seer came drifting back to him. He decided to investigate further. The young lady was by now out of sight but it seemed to Willie that she was one of a party of females which had been on its way to the beach. He proceeded at a lively pace until he found the party once more within his ken. It consisted of five members. He followed at a discreet distance, not wishing to overplay his hand and thus destroy his chances altogether. The party descended a stone stairway to where an array of ancient bathing boxes stood facing the shimmering sea. There followed some brief negotiations with the proprietor after which the five took possession of a similar number of the rust-wheeled wooden structures.

Willie Ramley carefully noted the box into which his Lady Fair had disappeared. There was nothing for it but to wait until she came out. A strange sensation began to assail him, a composition of excitement and expectancy. He guessed that the five were country folk. He deduced this from the way in which they had looked around and about when they arrived at their destination. It was also apparent from their simple apparel and the way they carried themselves that they were daughters of the soil. He had expected a chaste emergence from the bathing boxes but he was totally unprepared for the sight which met his eyes. Each of the five was decked out in a long shift which fell to the toes and which concealed all the shapeliness thereunder. The shifts were off-white in color and the material lightweight. What Willie Ramley could not know was that these full-length costumes were the common bathing attire of the people of the countryside. Thrifty souls that they were, these frugal females rarely visited emporiums for the material which went into the making of their underclothes and beach attire. The flour which was used for the making of the daily bread came, as a rule, in calico bags of one hundred and twelve pounds or one hundredweight. When the flour was used up the bags were thoroughly washed and dried. The textile was used to make shifts, slips and knickers, not to mention football togs and bedclothes. While the numerous town and city people on the beach might regard the calico-clad countrywomen with some amusement they, nevertheless, refrained from showing it. This could well be because they themselves had only recently emerged from country backgrounds.

Despite the lack of design, the shifts sat well on their owners as they moved in stately formation from bathing boxes to shore with their heads held high to show how little they cared about what others thought. Their leader was a formidable, mightily-busted lady of late middle years, tall and broad-shouldered with aquiline features and a bearing which suggested that she was capable of defending herself and her charges in the unlikely event of an attack. The others were younger by far, late teens or early twenties so that Willie could not be blamed for concluding that the matriarch was more than likely the mother of the four. They walked demurely behind her, looking neither left nor right. The girl who had prevented Willie's collision with the bus brought up the rear and it was clear that, under the shapeless shift, there was a body as beautiful as the imagination could conjure up. Reaching the water, they proceeded along its edge to a spot where no other human soul was in evidence. Here, prompted by the matron, the young ladies entered the sea and, after much skipping, leaping and shrieking, accustomed themselves to its cold but salving wavelets. Then, dutifully, while the matron kept a look-out in the background, the four faced themselves to the distant horizon and lifting the fronts of their shifts liberally sprinkled the exposed part of the anatomy with handfuls of cleansing sea water. The matron herself did not enter the water at all, content in her role of mother hen, repelling the curious with the most intimidatory of looks and doughty of stances. As soon as the girls had finished, they chastely lowered their shifts and turned their backs to the very same horizon. The first exercise was repeated until the matron was satisfied that each was adequately bathed. Mustering her charges in a single file, she resumed her position at the head of the column. Proudly and gracefully, they returned the way they had come. Willie Ramley decided to make a closer inspection. He strode seawards with what he hoped was a casual air, pouting his lips into an indifferent whistle, giving the impression that he was an innocent holidaymaker lost in a private world of his own. Warily he circled round the matriarch as she led her brood to the boxes. His aim was to keep pace with the group from the rear so that he could better observe the lady of his choice. As he neared completion of his arc their eyes met ever so fleetingly but in that split-second exchange he lost his heart irrevocably. Again he recalled the seer's advice, "Do not let yourself be carried away by a pretty face."

There was more, however, to this young lady than a pretty face. Of that he was certain. He fell in behind and then he saw for the first time the word "Sunrise" imprinted in faded red letters on the back of the shift. Willie Ramley would have had no way of knowing that this was the brand name of the popular variety of flour greatly favored by the country folk of the time. The letters were in large capitals and underneath there was a longer inscription in faded black italics.

Anxious to acquaint himself with its contents he closed the gap between them until the lettering was easily legible. "One hundred and twelve pounds," it said, "guaranteed pure."

He repeated the words over and over again to himself but it was only when the object of his interest had disappeared into her bathing box that the full significance of the latter part of the seer's advice impressed itself upon him. What was that he had said again, something about a special mark or sign that would set his wife-to-be apart. But what were the precise words? Slowly they came back to him.

"There will be something about her . . . It will be as clear as though it were stamped upon her back." Those were the exact words as far as he could recall. No further evidence of the girl's character was needed. He waited impatiently for her re-emergence.

For the remainder of his holiday, Willie Ramley embarked upon a consistent and most earnest suit. Morning, noon and night he waited upon her. The girl's mother was impressed by his undeviating devotion and when, at length, Willie had prevailed upon the young lady to say yes, the mother approved unreservedly and the pair were married. The honeymoon, as was to be expected, was spent in Ballybunion and on the first night of what turned out to be a most blessed union the blushing bride presented herself to her husband clad in nothing but the long shift which carried on its back the inscription: "One hundred and twelve pounds. Guaranteed pure." And indeed it must be said here that never was a product so truthfully advertised.

"The Teapots Are Out"

"I was present," Dinny Colman boasted, "the day the first shot was fired."

"It wasn't a shot, was it?" my mother prompted, noticing my bewilderment.

"Of course it wasn't," Dinny replied, "but in all wars household or otherwise, someone has to start things off. The wrong word in the wrong place at the wrong time will do just as nicely or suppose people was taking their supper and if someone was to get fat meat who didn't like fat meat while others who didn't care whether they got fat or lean was presented with lean that would do it. I seen it happen. It may seem a small thing but in the eyes of the victim a great wrong has been done. A man's supper has been destroyed and in this God-forsaken countryside a man's supper is about the only diversion he has before drawing the clothes over his head for the night."

He flicked the reins and called "Giddap!" The bobbing rump twitched. The ears pricked. The paces stretched and quickened. The wind sang in our ears and we had to raise our voices to be heard. We were traveling on the flat. It wasn't till the pace slowed as we climbed the first of the forbidding hills on the road homeward that I found the composure to ponder Dinny's remarks.

The house we had just left was a thatched, one-story farmhouse like our own. Indeed it was like every other farmhouse in the countryside with the difference that on the one we had lately vacated the thatch was hoary and rotten, retaining not a glimmer of the rich burnished yellow which it once boasted. The white-washed walls were long since brown-stained by the stinking, blackened rainwater which oozed and seeped from the reeking thatch. The small, deep-set windows afforded little or no light to the interior. Add to this the fact that they had not been cleaned for years save where the imprint of a palm had smoothed a lookout from which occasional visitors might be vetted. The run-down farm had been let year after year to a neighbor while the byroad from the main road to the house was no longer distinguishable from the rushy fields through which it ran. Famished, underfed bullocks stood waiting for hay in a large bawling herd just inside the main gate. They looked as if they hadn't eaten for days! The general picture was one of casual decay.

"The teapots was out when we landed and out when we left." Dinny was speaking to my mother.

The farm was owned by Neddy Leary. With him in the kitchen during our visit had been his wife Dolly and his sister Bridgeen. Because they had been partaking of some afternoon tea, we had surprised them. Each was seated at a different table, Neddy at the large, main table which stood in the center of the kitchen, his wife and sister at either side of the turf fire which smoldered under a large, black iron kettle. Each had wet and drawn their separate pots of tea and withdrawn with them to their respective positions. Bread, milk, butter and sugar were communal and could be had from an appointed area at the end of the main table. The remaining space was restricted, the preserve of Neddy Leary. In truth the smaller tables were no more than glorified butter boxes which had been upturned and covered with patches of spare tarpaulin.

We had heard the sounds of discord quite plainly as we neared the house. All three were involved. It had reached hysterical proportions just as my mother knocked upon the door. Suddenly there wasn't a titter to be heard. A grimy face appeared at the window and, shortly afterwards, a voice called, "Come in." By this time, however, Dinny Colman, who was never a man to stand on ceremony, had the door open. The disarray was quite evident.

"God bless all here," he used the benediction to camouflage his extreme curiosity. Hastily, Dolly Leary and her sister-in-law Bridgeen departed the hearth, clutching their teapots and other relevant accoutrements. They disappeared soundlessly into an adjacent room.

"Come in, come in," Neddy Leary cried as though there had never been a word of disagreement. Dinny Colman made immediately for the hearth and stood with his back to it so that the whole kitchen could be kept more easily under observation.

"Servant boys don't know their place no more," Neddy Leary addressed himself to my mother, at the same time rising and ushering us both to the hearth where he bade us sit on the chairs which had just been abandoned. This left Dinny with no choice but to move to one side. Using heavy black tongs, Neddy Leary set himself the task of rearranging the turf fire. This he managed to do with a surprising degree of skill. In seconds, it was a tastefully-constructed pile of glowing embers, quite pleasant to behold and radiating welcome warmth. He delicately banked it with sods chosen from an ancient tea-chest which stood nearby. He declined, however, to sweep the hearth and surrounds clean of ashes. He managed to give the impression that this was a chore beneath his dignity.

"As soon as that kettle boils," he politely informed my mother, "we'll wet a mouthful of tea and discuss your business."

Having said this, his face hardened and he called out in a loud voice, "Come down here this instant." As he once more turned to my mother, the harshness left his face. "They'll be down now to set the table," he told her. Meanwhile Dinny Colman had moved nearer the door where he made a thorough investigation of that makeshift portal. He seemed determined to record every contrary detail. He moved next to the farthest corner overhead which was a hen-coop covered by lattice wire. Several pullets and hens of the Rhode Island Red species sat contentedly staring into space as though drugged or dazed. Reaching upward, Dinny thrust a finger though the lattice and tapped the nearest of the hens on its beak. There followed a soft, fruity clucking.

"Let those hens be!" The order came from Neddy Leary. He had been noting Dinny's progress with mounting displeasure. Dinny moved on to where a picture of the Sacred Heart was barely visible through a cracked, dust-covered glass frame. He took a deep breath and expeled it in the direction of the picture. His every action was a deliberate manifestation of his amusement.

Dolly Leary was the first to arrive from the room. "You know my woman, don't you?" Neddy said.

"Indeed I do," my mother answered. Nevertheless, she shook hands with Dolly who looked far tidier now than when we first entered.

After a few moments, enough to allow Dolly establish herself, Bridgeen Leary presented herself. "And my sister," Neddy said. Again there was a handshake.

"Will ye take an egg with the tea?" Neddy enquired and he lifted a black canister with the tongs. It was half-filled with murky water, the surface of which was partly covered with ashes.

"No, thanks," the three of us answered hastily, too hastily. My mother made amends by stating that we had partaken of our dinners just before we set out. Dolly and Bridgeen began to clear the table. They were watched closely by Dinny who had returned to resume a less familiar form of communication with the Rhode Island Reds. Between them, the women of the house managed to spirit away all the unsightly objects which had first greeted us. In no time at all, a tablecloth covered the table. There were cups and saucers, side plates and a large dish which contained an outsize pancake and the quarter of a currant loaf.

"Dang that kettle," Neddy Leary said but, just as he spoke, the faint curling steam from its spout was suddenly transformed into a solid jet. He took himself to the table where a whispered consultation took place between himself and the two women. The argument concerned itself with which of the three teapots should be used for the occasion. One word borrowed another and it seemed as if the parley might erupt into a major row. Suddenly there was silence. An agreement had been reached. Dolly Leary raced to the room she had just left and returned at once with a brown earthenware teapot which was obviously being pressed into service for the first time. It was quickly rinsed with a gurgling squirt from the boiling kettle. Neddy arranged a circle of small coals of a uniform size a few inches from the fire and on these the freshly-made tea in its brand new teapot was allowed to draw. While we waited,

Dolly and Bridgeen made the joint observation that I was like my father but had my mother's eyes. Meanwhile, in the hen-coop there was uproar. Dinny, the party responsible, had quickly removed himself from the scene of the crime and was once again inspecting the door.

"Take a seat at once, sir," Neddy spoke curtly and indicated a chair at the bottom of the table. Suspecting that a limit might have been reached, Dinny sat at once. One by one we joined him at the table. Neither of the household women sat till the tea had been poured. Neddy sliced the pancake and the currant loaf. A tell-tale, off-white vein ran through each of the pancake slices. In the case of the currant loaf, the fruit had sunk to the bottom. Despite this, we would be obliged to partake of at least one slice. Thereafter, it would be possible to decline all pressure to eat more. Gingerly, we opted for the currant loaf. It was heavy going. No crumb fell to the table or the floor, such was its soggy consistency. We managed to get it down, however, and so placed ourselves in a position to refuse all other offers. The household, having satisfied itself that our wants were fulfilled, ate heartily until nothing remained in the dish.

"Now," Neddy Leary announced as he wiped his mouth with the back of his hand, "tell us what it was that brought ye."

"Not much," my mother answered, "just to find out if you could give us your brother Tom's address in New York."

"With a heart and a half, but tell us who belonging to you is for America?"

"This boy here," my mother informed him.

"He's young, isn't he?"

"Old enough at sixteen," my mother responded.

Neddy Leary sighed. "The best age," he agreed. "They don't settle so well when they shove on in the years. That was Tom's age when he left. Never looked back. Made out fine for himself."

Neddy's younger brother Tom figured as a sort of intercessory between prospective American employers and the droves of young Irish boys and girls who emigrated yearly from the district. It was a genuine labor of love on his behalf and indeed it would be unthinkable for any intending emigrant not to contact him before leaving. His house served as a home from home during those heartbreaking first weeks. It gave the youngsters a chance to absorb the strange, complex environment until such time as they were able to make some slight evaluation of the new situation for themselves.

"I'll get it for you right away," Neddy said. He rose and entered another room to the left of the kitchen. Nobody spoke during his absence. My mother cleared her throat and was about to say something but changed her mind. Dinny Colman eased himself self-consciously out of his chair and betook himself to the hearth where he first looked up the sooty chimney before standing with his behind to the fire, hands behind his back. He stood with a knowing smile on his face, his lips pursed, issuing a sly, soundless whistle. Neddy returned with a writing pad, a bottle of black ink and a small well-thumbed notebook.

Behind his ear was a wooden-handled pen with a rusty nib. His wife and sister cleared the table feverishly while he stood imperiously waiting behind his chair. His eyes scanned the table for signs of any object which might impair the work which was about to begin. When he sat, the two women stood in attendance directly behind him, no more than a foot apart. Even Dinny Colman was impressed by the ritual. He was made to feel that he was in the presence of a scribe. An inner sense told him that it was not a moment for levity. Laboriously Neddy Leary laid out his writing materials on the table. When he was settled properly in his chair, he uncorked the ink bottle, having first held it up to the light for careful inspection in case it harbored any foreign bodies. Satisfying himself in this respect, he next inspected the rusty nib. Not finding it to his satisfaction, he thrust it into his mouth, twirling it round and round several times therein and then proceeded to suck it as though it were a lollipop. Removing it, he held it close to his eyes for final inspection. He dried it by the simple expedient of rubbing it against the sleeve of his coat. He then wet the thumb of his right hand with his tongue, lifted the notebook eye-high and thumbed through its tattered pages until a deep sigh of satisfaction intimated that he had found what he had been looking for.

"Thomas Ignatius Augustine Leary," he chanted the words with due solemnity. "Two forty-seven, East Two Sixty-second Street, City of New York, United States of America," he concluded with an American twang. He then carefully proceeded to copy the address onto the notepaper.

As he wrote, not a pin could be heard to fall, a feather to alight, a heart to flutter, until he had almost completed his task. Quite out of the blue, you might say almost sacrilegiously, his sister Bridgeen covered part of her bosom with one hand and all of her mouth with the other before emitting a clearly audible gasp that shattered the concentration of the scribe as though a shotgun had been discharged over his head. His reaction was not to erupt from his chair mouthing blasphemous barrages in his sister's direction. He merely folded his hands while the color of his face changed to a ghastly hue. A nerve-jangling silence of several moments ensued. Neddy Leary closed his eyes and spoke.

"Is there somebody present with something to say?" His voice shook with emotion. It was evident that he was making mighty efforts to control himself.

"It was me made the noise," Bridgeen replied without a hint of apology in her voice.

"Why so?" Neddy was now drumming his fingers inquisitorially on the table.

"Because," said his sister sarcastically, "that's the old address." So flaring a transgression was this that it simply had to be ignored. To contradict the head of the house in the presence of strangers could not be brooked, no matter what. In the circumstances, the only alternative was to pretend the woman had not spoken. Without haste Neddy finished off the address, rose, held it to the fire and allowed the ink thereon to dry. While he was thus engaged, his wife committed the second cardinal error of the afternoon.

"If you're not careful, you'll burn it," she said. From the expression on his face, it was plain that Neddy had decided to treat this comment with the same detachment as the other. When the ink had dried he folded the sheet of notepaper and handed it to my mother. His hands trembled and a furious fire burned in his dark eyes.

"I wish the boy luck," he said gently, "and now if you have no further business you might like to be shortening your road."

"Of course," my mother agreed, "and let me thank you for your kindness."

A sensitive woman, she could readily presage the signs of the approaching storm. Any moment now, the lightning would flash and the thunder roll and crack. The barely restrained winds of rage were already rustling dangerously. One could almost run one's fingers over the bristling tension.

"Time to go," my mother ushered me to the door which Neddy Leary had obligingly opened for us. As ever Dinny Colman was inclined to dawdle. He posed affectedly in the doorway as though admiring the landscape while all he really wanted was to savor the beginnings of the oncoming conflict. He savored it all right but not in the manner he would have liked. Behind him stood Neddy Leary waiting to close the door so that he might give rein to his anger. When Dinny refused to budge, Neddy drew back his right foot and forcefully impressed the side of his boot on Dinny's buttocks, making him to buck forward unceremoniously till he found himself on all fours. As soon as the kick was implanted, Neddy banged the door shut, the better to begin the domestic dissension in earnest. Outside, after Dinny had recovered, we marveled at the indoor commotion. The first shot was fired in this instance when the ink bottle came flying through the window. Then came the clangor of human voices upraised and distorted till they seemed inhuman. It was a wanton, reckless, irascible strife. There was the sound of splintering wood mingled with the crash of breaking crockery. Add to this the noisome jangle of canisters, pannies, buckets and other tin missiles and some idea of the general bedlam will be conveyed.

The climax came with a mighty crash followed by the terrified clucking of badly-maimed hens. The hen-coop had fallen; whether by accident or design we could not determine. Suddenly there was silence. The battle was over. The door opened and a file of Rhode Islanders staggered and limped out from the scene of the fray. In the kitchen Neddy Leary sat at the table with his head in his hands. His wife and sister sat holding their sides at either side of the hearth. A lifeless hen lay sprawled on the floor. There was debris everywhere.

"Come along," my mother said, "they'll need to be alone now."

"The teapots will be out forever after this," Dinny Colman forecasted. He was still peeved at the way he had been treated by Neddy Leary. Reluctantly, he followed us to the pony and trap. As we climbed the second hill Dinny was still muttering to himself over the injustice which had been done to him.

"Tell us about the very first shot," I said. He mulled over the suggestion for a while.

"I worked there at the time," he began. "It was a fine place, carrying twenty milch cows and two score of dry stock. There was only the pair of them, Neddy and the sister. Tom had gone to the States to make his fortune. Neddy one night took it into his head to carry Dolly Mack home from a dance in the village. He made a habit of the thing after that and it was no time at all before the pair decided to marry. The trouble started the second day after the marriage. We were after coming in from the meadow. The new wife laid the table and put the eggs on to boil. Bridgeen sat near the fire darning a sock. Things was quiet and peaceful.

"Will you eat one egg or two?" Dolly asked of Neddy.

"Two, if you please," said he.

"Will you eat one egg or two?" she says to me.

"Two, if you please," said I.

"Will you eat one egg or two?" she says to Bridgeen Leary, her sister-in-law.

"Will I eat my own eggs, is it?" she threw back at Dolly. That was the first shot to be fired between the two and of course Neddy was soon drawn into it. The teapots came out soon after that and from the looks of things today they'll stay out for all time."

Under the Sycamore Tree

Jimmy Bowen was by no means fastidious, yet every evening he would shave and wash meticulously before donning his best clothes in preparation for his trip to the river side. Having left the house he would stand in front of the shop window and take careful stock of himself. Should there be the slightest evidence of disorder anywhere on his person he would re-enter the house straightaway and set about correcting the imperfection. Having satisfied himself that every possible step had been taken regarding the reorganization of his appearance he would present himself a second time to the shop window. Often he would stand there for several minutes pretending to be engrossed in a study of the window's contents whereas he was really searching for flaws in his appearance. When he was satisfied that no further improvement could be effected, he would set off on his walk. The time he chose varied from season to season but always it would be roughly a half hour before darkness fell. First he would stroll leisurely through the streets before arriving at the laneway which led to the river side path. The moment he sighted the water his features underwent a change. His eyes grew brighter. His ears seemed to prick as though he were alerting himself for an exciting encounter. He became a different person.

At sixty, Jimmy Bowen was a spare, gray-haired, lively man who moved with an athlete's facility. He was well off. Rumor had it that he never married because the girl he loved was killed in a car accident or drowned or worse. Nobody was quite clear. He had left the town in his late teens and returned twenty years later to take over the family hardware business when his father was taken ill. He had never seen eye to eye with the old man although they had never lost touch or so it was said. When the elder Bowen died, Jimmy assumed control. His mother passed on shortly afterwards and it seemed inevitable that he would take a wife. He was young enough. A fit man of forty with his reputed means should have no trouble. He remained single, however, and was the bane of the town's over-blossomed spinsters for several years. At sixty, with his hair whitened by the years, he was no longer regarded as a candidate for the marriage stakes. His business prospered and there was much conjecture as to what would happen when he grew too old to carry on. He had a first cousin in a distant town, a ne'er-do-well with a large brood. Jimmy was persuaded by friends of the family that it would be an act of charity to bring the oldest boy into the business. It hadn't worked. The lad knew it all from the outset. He disappeared one day with several hundred pounds and was heard of no more.

The river side path which was the route of Jimmy's evening strolls was flanked on the one side by giant oaks and sycamores and on the other by the wide sweep of the river bank. It was a picturesque walk less frequented now than at any time in its history. Lovers no longer dallied there, preferring to speed through the countryside in motor cars. Older people, unless the weather was exceptionally fine, chose to sit and watch television. Consequently, the only people Jimmy Bowen met were the occasional fowler and fisherman. This was the way he liked it even though it must be said that he entertained other secret aspirations. His favorite time was when darkness descended. To celebrate this delicate event, he would stand unmoving under a favorite sycamore. It was best when no breezes blew. On these occasions of tranquillity he would stand entranced, utterly absorbed by what was happening. Sometimes the motionless lineaments of the river would be mottled with infinitesimal flecks of foam. Even the birds would be hushed. It would be that precise time of evening when light resigns itself to half light yielding finally to darkness and it seemed all nature was aware that consummate stillness was required if an honorable surrender was to take place. This was the very time when Jimmy Bowen longed for fulfilment of his secret aspirations. Quite simply, what he hoped for was that a woman, the woman of his dreams, might emerge from the river side shadows and stand by his side to share in the romantic transition. It was, he knew, more than he was entitled to expect in such a place and at such a time. When, as always, she failed to materialize, he would return the way he had come, still cherishing the notion that she might appear before him out of one of the many bowers and groves along the way. At the back of his mind was the certainty that she would appear one evening. She would just happen to be there and that would be that. When it happened, he would take her hand and they would return together towards the lights of the town. Words would be unnecessary.

The cold truth was that for twenty years Jimmy had returned to the town empty-handed but this had not succeeded in putting a damper on his expectations. He was as hopeful as ever. In the shop, he worked with such earnest endeavor that no onlooker could possibly credit that the man's private life was founded on such improbable romantic notions. The very opposite would seem to be far more likely. His staff consisted of two counter-hands, middle-aged brothers who had started their apprenticeships with his father. There was a federal factotum, an elderly fellow, another relict from his father's tenure and there was Miss Miller. It would be difficult to determine Miss Miller's exact age. Mousy Miller the customers called her. She had joined the staff at the time of his father's illness and spent her working hours in an elevated glass office where she could command a view of every corner of the shop. She dressed chastely, wore spectacles and rarely used make-up. She had few friends and seemed content to spend most of her free time with her landlady, an elderly widow. Originally, she hailed from the midlands. Her people, it was believed, were modest farmers. Jimmy rarely entered the office. When he did, it was at Miss Miller's invitation. She always stood when he entered and allowed him to take the seat which she had just vacated. Usually the visit would consist of inspecting a contractor's account which might have exceeded the stipulated limit or to discuss the necessity for consulting a solicitor over other unpaid accounts of long standing. She always called him Mr. Bowen. He never called her anything but Miss Miller. Although he never objected to these occasional conferences he always felt that his presence was superfluous. She might appear to be mousy and effete but her knowledge of the business was astonishingly comprehensive. The books were immaculately kept. At a moment's notice she could provide an exact run-down of the firm's financial standing for any period. It was she who dealt with the auditors, saw to the stocktaking and staff bonuses, made up the weekly wage packets and took on the hundred and one other minor tasks which contributed to the running of a successful business. It could be said that she knew her employer inside out. Jimmy knew her worth and paid her accordingly. Ask anywhere in the town and you would be told that, whatever else, Jimmy Bowen was first and foremost a decent man.

He had a somewhat different relationship with the rest of the staff. A casual customer would be hard put to know who was boss and who was counterhand. It worked well. The country people who patronized the shop liked a man without pretension, a man who would sit on the counter and pass the time of day. He had other traits which appealed to townspeople and country people alike. The chief of these was his tendency to take off on the occasional skite. He never took a conventional holiday. When the urge caught him, an urge which generally coincided with a fine spell, he would betake himself to the office pay slot and indicate his financial requirements to Miss Miller.

"Slip us a few hundred," he might say. The money, in fivers and tenners, would be forthcoming at once without comment of any kind from Miss Miller.

"See you in a few days," he would say as soon as the notes were pocketed. Home then to change into slacks, pullover and sandals. Garage next for a petrol fill and a hasty check of elementals. Thence to the nearest city or, if the season was right, to a distant holiday resort. His customers received news of these breaks with amusement. They knew the drill or thought they did. There had to be a woman or women. Why else would he go on his own? A good man's case this. Not even a step-mother would blame him. Many envied him the manner in which he took off in the first place. He needed nobody's permission and best of all he could come back when it suited him. On his return he never tendered the least information as to how he had fared, a sure sign this, his friends said, that a debauch had taken place.

The truth was that Jimmy Bowen did no more than sleep out in the mornings. The remainder of the day he spent inspecting the neighborhood pubs and hotels. Sometimes he drank on his own. Other times he joined up with single gentlemen like himself or became involved in sing-songs. By midnight it would be as much as he could do to locate his room under his own steam. This then was the pattern of his respite. There had never been any serious involvement with a woman. He remained faithful to his river side fantasies and would fall into a happy if drunken sleep recalling the enchanting images of his favorite place or endeavoring to trace the shadowy features of the lovely creature who had thus far failed to realize herself from the place in question. Always he slept soundly, not waking till the chambermaids knocked on his door at a time when the morning was well advanced. He never surfaced before noon. By the time he had read through the morning papers, lunch would have become available. Having partaken, he would sit for a while before indulging in the only physical exercise of the day. This consisted of an hour-long stroll after which he felt free to indulge himself in the first drink of the day. After a sojourn of four to five days, his appetite for change would be sated and he would return home.

There would be no drink on the day of the homecoming. He also made a point of arriving at the shop after dark. After a snack, he would make straight for his bed where he stayed until the effects of the prolonged booze had worn off. As a rule, this took no more than a sleep out until the late afternoon of the following day when he would arise refreshed and ready to resume his normal way of life. This was not to say that he was abstemious between skites. Most nights after returning from the river, he stopped off at the Anglers' Rest where he allowed himself a whiskey or two before polishing off a few pints of draft stout. He never drank alone. There was always a crony or two in attendance and invariably he joined up with these until time was called.

Shortly after his sixtieth birthday, he embarked upon the longest and most intensive skite of his career. He departed the town early on Monday afternoon and was not seen again in its vicinity for a period of ten days. What transpired during that time will never be fully revealed. Even with the aid of Miss Miller, if Jimmy Bowen ever endeavored to itemize the events which took place, the task would be impossible for the excellent reason that they were beyond recall. To be more accurate, it could be said that they had foundered irrevocably in an alcoholic haze. Occasionally, in later years, glimpses of that foggy interlude would be borne back to him but none of sufficient duration or clarity to enlighten him. It was, as he intimated to his cronies not long after his return, the father and mother of all skites and the cronies, to give them their due, accepted this evaluation without question. Jimmy Bowen was not a man to exaggerate. There was no doubt that he had been on the skite of a lifetime. What he did remember, most vividly at that, was waking up on the final day. His head throbbed with a pain so over-powering that he despaired of ever facing the world again. For hours, he tossed and turned on the bed. Towards late afternoon, he steeled himself with every ounce of resolve at his disposal and entered the bathroom. He filled the bath with cold water and stood nearby in his pelt waiting for it to fill. This will kill me or cure me, he told himself. He did not ease himself into the water. It might be said that he plopped in. He screamed when the first shock assailed him. Having barely survived it, he shuddered and spluttered like a man demented as the cold touched every part of his body. Despairingly, he started to sing. His voice trembled and shook. He could not sustain a single note no matter how hard he tried. There was one fearful moment when he felt totally paralysed. Panic-stricken, he erupted from the bath and landed on his behind on the slippery floor. Rising laboriously, he dried himself thoroughly. After a few minutes, he felt an improvement. His head still throbbed but the pain was now bearable. His hands were steady. He decided to risk a shave. Surprisingly, he negotiated the business without a nick. He combed his hair and sat on the bed. He had no idea where he was. He was about to lift the phone when it occurred to him that he was naked. Hastily, he pulled on his trousers. There was still some money in the fob; he was surprised at the amount. Probably cashed a check or two.

All would be revealed in due course as the man said. He lifted the receiver and waited.

"Good afternoon, Mister Bowen."

"Good afternoon. Where am I?"

A hearty girlish laugh from the other end.

"I'm serious. Where am I?"

"Poor Mister Bowen. I believe you."

"Well?"

"The Neptune."

"Galway?"

"Galway."

"Thanks." There was relief in his voice. Galway was less than three hours from home. He looked at his watch. Three forty-five. First he would eat something, pay his bill and then the road. He estimated that a leisurely speed should see him safely home with plenty of light in hand. He looked forward eagerly to the drive. At seven-thirty as he drove through the outskirts of his home town there was still no sign of darkness. Like the skite which he had just put behind him he would never be able to present a detailed or coherent account of what happened next. He decided that it was too bright to go straight to the shop. Instead he headed for the Angler's Rest. The place was deserted save for the proprietress Mrs. Malone.

"You're back," she said as though he had been away no longer than usual. There had in fact been mounting speculation all the week about his whereabouts. This had been replaced by genuine concern. In fact his cronies had decided to take the matter up with the civic guards should he fail to show up at the weekend. A skite was a skite but there were limits.

"Did you have a nice time?" Mrs. Malone asked, hoping that the excitement did not show in her voice.

"Tip top," Jimmy assured her. "Let's have a glass of Jameson, will you?"

While she dispensed the order, Mrs. Malone considered which of Jimmy's cronies and which of her own friends she would ring first. Collecting the note which he had tendered, she excused herself, ostensibly to look for change. She made several phone calls, at the same time keeping an eye on Jimmy from the back lounge where the phone was located. She conveyed each individual disclosure in a tone that was little above a whisper. Jimmy sat silently sipping his whiskey, unaware of what was going on. It had not occurred to him that his prolonged absence might have generated disquiet. All his thoughts were concentrated in an effort to determine the rate at which the daylight was fading outside.

"All too soon," he told himself, "it will be dark." Suddenly he rose. He had reached a decision. It was time for his visit to the river. The whiskey had left him groggy but it had also brought a welcome warmth. In this happy state, he departed the Anglers' Rest and sauntered, at leisure, to the river side. Twilight hung between the river and the sky. In all too short a time, darkness would envelop the scene and the magical fleeting moments of transition would be no more. Already the shadows were expanded to their fullest. Any moment now, the last pale threads of evening would vanish into the dark tapestry of night. Jimmy Bowen proceeded apace towards his favorite tree. The world stood still or so it seemed. The mottled water moved soundlessly on. Jimmy Bowen stopped, arrested in his tracks by what seemed to be a female form standing under the wide branches of the sycamore. His heart fluttered. His breathing quickened. He peered prayerfully through the half-light, advancing slowly. There was no mistaking the form. It was definitely that of a woman. A flimsy headscarf adorned her averted head. A white mackintosh covered her slender frame. This cannot be, Jimmy Bowen told himself and yet the creature is there, living and breathing as sure as darkness is descending. He harrumphed delicately lest he startle her. She turned suddenly and in a thrice she was in his arms. All at once, Jimmy Bowen knew that something huge, something altogether monumental had been missing from his life until that moment. The embrace lasted an eternity or so Jimmy thought. In reality, it ended after half a minute. He dared not look at her face. He risked a hasty glance and was pleased with what he saw in the darkness. Her features were somewhat angular but pleasantly defined. A solitary tear or what he took to be a tear glistened on her cheek under the weak moonlight. This was to be expected. They had both waited for too long a time. He was equally overcome even if there was no tear to prove it. Gently he took her by a hand that melted immediately into his. Slowly they returned along the way he had come. Mrs. Malone looked up apprehensively when the door opened. She always did. A pub was a pub and you never knew when a troublemaker might put in an appearance. The relief showed on her face when Jimmy Bowen entered. This was wiped away altogether and replaced by genuine amazement when she beheld his companion.

"Sweet, Sacred Heart," she addressed her customers, "'tis Mousy Miller and she without her specs."

All within earshot turned to stare. A hush fell over the bar. Mrs. Malone allowed her eyes to focus on Jimmy Bowen. There was a sort of glow to him. He still stood beside the doorway in a total trance, Miss Miller by his side. It was as though they were waiting for somebody to direct them. There was a word somewhere for the way Jimmy Bowen looked. Mrs. Malone could not bring it to mind at once. Moonstruck, that was it, moonstruck.

After a while one of Jimmy's cronies arose and located seats for the pair.

"I declare but she looks downright attractive," Mrs. Malone confided to the customer nearest her. "A bit too much make-up maybe but, still and for all, attractive. You'd hardly know her."

At the counter, Jimmy dawdled happily for a moment or two.

"I'll have a Jameson," he said.

"And Miss Miller?" Mrs. Malone put the question.

"Miss Miller?"

"Behind you."

Jimmy Bowen turned slowly and directed all his fading energies towards a hard look at his companion.

"Dammit if she isn't a dead ringer for Miss Miller." He

threw the observation over his shoulder to Mrs. Malone.

"Ask her what she's having." Mrs. Malone's exasperation was beginning to show. Still Jimmy refused to budge. He just stood there with his back to the counter, happily, if perplexedly, contemplating his new-found love.

"What are you having, dear?" Mrs. Malone called.

"Sweet sherry if you please," came the demure and immediate reply.

"Dammit if she don't talk like her as well." For the first time a note of alarm registered in Jimmy's voice. It conveyed itself immediately to Miss Miller. She looked about shamefacedly.

"Dammit," Jimmy Bowen was saying as he looked at her from another angle, "it is Miss Miller. Why didn't somebody tell me?" He looked foolishly from one watching face to another. An awesome silence had descended. Everybody looked everywhere, at Jimmy Bowen and Mrs. Malone, at one another, at the ceiling, everywhere but at Miss Miller.

"Excuse me," it was no more than a whisper but it was heard in every corner of the bar. It came from Miss Miller. She was on her feet.

"Your sherry." Mrs. Malone proffered the offering too late. Miss Miller was already on her way to the door which she closed gently behind her. There followed a short period of uneasy silence. Then came the clamor of relief. Everyone spoke at the same time. Jimmy Bowen alone was silent. He seemed dumbfounded. On his face was a look of utter perplexity. Still reeling, he walked slowly towards the door. For an hour or more, he walked aimlessly through the streets. Slowly, painfully, sobriety returned to him. Eventually he found himself at his own shop window. He fumbled for his keys while he took stock of his reflection. He looked none the worse for wear, eyes a little tell-tale maybe, face a little drawn, white hair a little tousled yet, all in all, presentable enough. He located the appropriate key but could not bring himself to insert it in the lock. He stood undecided, weighing the keys in his palm, considering his reflection. He closed his eyes firmly and opened them again. This time he looked beyond the reflection. Slowly, in his mind, a hazy background of trees and river water began to take shape. Out of the darkening landscape, a pair of human forms, male and female, their features as yet indiscernible, emerged side by side from the shadows and stood under the sycamore. Jimmy Bowen held his breath as the female form gracefully inclined its head in his direction. The radiant smile on Miss Miller's face was for Jimmy Bowen and Jimmy Bowen alone. This was beyond dispute. Her heart showed clearly on her face. It sang for Jimmy Bowen.

"Why not?" he asked aloud. "Why not?" he asked turning from the window and addressing himself to the street at large. "Why not?" he asked of the stars overhead, "why not, why not, why not?" he asked as he hastened to the widow's house where Miss Miller sat inside her window with a tear in her eye.

Thrift

It was his father's miserliness that killed John Cutler. That's what the neighbors said afterwards. That was what Mick Kelly the postman said and Mick knew the Cutlers better than anybody. His cottage stood at the entrance to their farm. When John Cutler reached his thirty-fifth year, he confronted his father with the fact that he was at the halfway stage in his life's span with nothing to show for it.

"A few more years," he complained, "and I'll be an old man."

His father nodded but did not otherwise commit himself.

"I have a notion of getting married." He threw the bait out hopefully but the older man refused to rise to it.

While John stood waiting for some expression of sympathy or approval, his mother entered the kitchen. At once, she sensed there was a showdown in progress. She busied herself by the fireplace, silently praying that her industry would exempt her from taking sides.

"What do you expect me to do?" Tom Cutler rose from his chair and went to the open door where he absently surveyed the distant hills.

"You could sign over the place," John suggested.

"Can't do that. Damn well you know I can't do that."

"But why not?"

"Why not he asks and he knowing well. What's to become of your mother and me if you bring another woman in here?"

"Ye can have a room."

"A room, eh! A whole room to ourselves! And what about our feeding and a bit of money?"

"There will be guarantees in the agreement. The solicitor will see to that."

"And will the solicitor be here every day to see that the guarantees are carried out? There is no way I would allow another woman in here without five thousand pounds. I'd also want a separate dwelling on the land, nothing fancy, mind you, just a simple cot for two. That's not asking a lot now, is it?"

John threw his hands upwards in a gesture of total despair. "Where would I get five thousand pounds," he cried out angrily, "and the money to build a house?"

"If your future wife had a fortune it would help."

"My future wife, as you call her, has no money."

"You could borrow," the old man said.

"I couldn't," John told him, "not that kind of money; a few thousand yes but not what you ask."

Tom Cutler shrugged his shoulders. "It's tough," he said, "but I have to think of myself and your mother. If I don't, nobody else will. That's been proved a thousand times over. Now, if you've finished, you might do down and turn in the cows."

"So, that's to be the end of it, is it? My future is on the line and you want me to turn in the cows. Have you no more to say to me?"

"What more is there to say except that you have yourself to thank for the way you are today."

"Myself to thank!" the words exploded from John's mouth.

"Oh, now, face up to the truth, my boy. You didn't miss a night in the pub these last fifteen years."

"Oh, come off it," John shouted. "A few pints was the most I ever had and the beggars on the road had that."

"A few pints every night," his father pointed out, "is a lot of pints come the end of the week. A thrifty man would have a nice pile put by at this time of his life."

"What could I put by out of the miserable few pounds you paid me? After a packet of cigarettes and a drink there was nothing left. Nothing." He spat out the words and brushed by his father with clenched fists.

"Drink and cigarettes, sure recipes for poverty," the old man flung the words after him like stones after a worthless hound. He stood silently for a long while in the doorway. Then he turned to his wife.

"What do you make of that?" he asked. They were a wizened pair, looking older by far than their years. Both had sallow, pinched faces, stooped frames and decaying teeth. They presented an overall picture of neglect and want.

"I don't know what to say," Minnie Cutler responded.

Tom shook his head at the outrageousness of it all.

"Do you think he has a woman itself?" he asked.

"I don't think so," she answered after a while, "leastways not a regular one."

"I thought as much. All he wants is to get his hands on the place, then drink it out."

"Maybe if you were to give it over to him he'd come by a woman. No one will take with him unless the place is his own."

"I can't do that. We both know it won't work."

"But we have enough, Tom. God knows how much you have in the banks."

"You couldn't have enough for this world, you foolish woman. When I go, the place will be his but, 'till that time, he'll draw his wage and dance to my tune. I broke my back for this place and so did you. He'll bide his time."

"I don't know, Tom." Minnie Cutler folded her arms.

"He's thirty-five. He's going to seed. Most men of his age have their own places or at least they have the handling of the money."

"It won't work, Minnie," Tom Cutler was adamant. "Look around you. Look what happened to them that signed over."

"Some have it good, Tom."

"God's sake, woman, will you not be codding yourself. They're only letting on to have it good. Most of them are prisoners in the homes they once owned."

"But isn't that the whole cause of the trouble, Tom? Those that bought houses in the town or rented rooms are content enough. It's only when you have two women under the one roof that the trouble starts."

"Do you want me to spend every penny I possess on a house. Is that it?"

"It needn't be big."

"Of course it needn't be big but the money will be big and we'll end up paupers depending on a daughter-in-law for handouts."

"If you signed over we'd have our old age pensions."

"Will you get it into your head, woman, that I will not sign over. Do you think I'm mad? You want me to part with all I have in this world with one stroke of a pen."

"You could go halves with him."

"Won't work. The place isn't big enough to support two families."

"Would you not tell him that you'd be prepared to sign over after a year or two?"

"No, I would not, nor after twenty years if I live that long. There's a bit of a want in that fellow. He's a man for the good times. All he wants is drink and fags and carousing."

"Still he's a good worker."

"Is he now and pray how do you think he'd fare without me managing the place?"

"A woman would manage it for him quick enough."

"This place calls for a thrifty man, a man that won't squander money foolishly. Let him wait. He'll appreciate it all the more when 'tis his. I'm away to the cows."

"Who's to say but you're right," Minnie Cutler conceded. Experience had taught her that it was prudent to concede ground which she knew she could not win anyway. Consequently, there was never conflict between them, at least not of late.

For years too, she had not mentioned his tight-fistedness. She took it for granted. According to him, there was never anything to spare for clothes or holidays or tidbits. He would always provide enough for the bare necessities but nothing more. In time she had stopped asking. It made for a peaceful atmosphere and in her estimation that was worth all the deprivation. Waste not, want not had been Tom Cutler's strategy from the day he assumed ownership of the farm. It had been heavily in debt. Minnie's modest fortune had not been enough to compensate but non-stop penny-pinching had. Now they had cash in the bank and the land was stocked to its capacity. As the money mounted, Tom would regularly repeat a phrase which he had coined the day he discovered he was out of the red. "Thrift won't lose," he would say, "because thrift can't lose." The logic of his composition appealed more and more to him as the years went by.

He was well aware that his neighbors and those who knew him further afield criticized him constantly for what he considered to be one of the great virtues. His parsimony had become something of a local joke. Those who conducted church gate collections for various charities would nudge each other when Tom Cutler approached. He never subscribed, no matter how worthy the cause. As soon as he had passed the collection tables, he would permit himself the faintest of smiles. He smiled purely and simply because he still had his money. That, to Tom Cutler, was a genuine cause for mirth. He really relished such incidents. They were the only luxuries in which he indulged.

His son John, on the other hand, was known as a decent type. He hadn't much, his neighbors said, but, by God, that much was yours if you wanted it.

"He didn't bring it from his father," Mick Kelly would say, "'tis from the grandfather he brought it, his father's father. Now there was your decent man. Give you the shirt off his back, he would."

Inevitably, these assessments of his son would be relayed back one way or another to Tom. They occasioned him many a smile. So John was like his grandfather, was he, the same grandfather who drank himself to death and mortgaged the farm up to the hilt, the same grandfather who couldn't call on a shilling to bury the wife who died prematurely from shame. Tom had been forced to surrender the few pounds he had saved through his teens to buy a cheap coffin and have High Mass said for his mother. It had been a bitter lesson. His father had shamed him into putting up the money. He resolved immediately after his mother's funeral that his financial standing would never be revealed to anybody again, not even to his wife. Oh, she knew he had money and she might guess rightly that it was a tidy bit but, in this respect, she would be close-mouthed because, no matter how much she might crave after a commodity, her need for security outweighed all else. From the start, she had wanted him to part with his money. First the curtains hadn't been good enough, then the furniture, then the wallpaper and inevitably the house itself. He had always heard her out patiently. He would put her off with promises but, as the years passed and he began to accumulate a little money, he was able to boast that his frugality was paying off. In time, she began to see that he had been right.

"Wouldn't we be in a nice way now," he often told her, "if I had given in."

He had another son Willie, a subcontractor in England. A thrifty man was Willie. On the day of his departure, Tom had handed him his fare and a ten pound note.

"If you have any sense," he warned him, "you'll not break that note needlessly. Put it aside and soon you'll have another to keep it company."

And how much had Willie today? Willie had plenty because he had listened. More important, nobody but

Willie himself knew how much Willie had. That was the trouble about possessing money. You might spend years saving it while your very own kin had no thought but to squander it while you'd say Jack Robinson.

John Cutler's attitude towards his parents changed dramatically after the confrontation. It had been his wont each night upon returning home from the pub to impart the latest gossip going the rounds and to give an account of the activities of the pub's patrons if such activities warranted it. His parents looked forward to this nightly report, especially his father although he never commented, whatever the content. He enjoyed it all the more because it cost nothing. They would have retired before his arrival but the bedroom door would be partly open in expectation.

Now there was no communication between them. Tom and Minnie were not unduly worried. He had sulked before but had come out of it after a few days. This time it was to be different. Weeks went by and then months until Tom closed the bedroom door to show that he didn't care. Around this time, John started to grow careless about his appearance. Frequently too, he came home drunk from the pub. Some mornings, he was unable to rise for the milking. Minnie grew worried when she over-heard him talking in his room. She relayed the news to Tom who put it down to drink.

"Wasn't I the wise man," he told her, "to hold on to what I had? Wouldn't we be in a nice way now depending on a drunkard?"

The rift became worse when John demanded an

increase in wages.

"What do you want it for?" his father asked curtly.

"I need it to keep pace," John answered patiently.

"To keep pace with what, the price of drink, is it?"

"There's more than drink gone up and well you know it. I need a new suit and a few shirts. My best shoes are beyond repair."

"Wait till the fall of the year," had been Tom Cutler's response. "I'll know better where I stand."

"And the rise?"

"I don't see what you need a rise for unless 'tis drink."

The old man had gone to the bedroom and locked himself in to avoid further argument. In despair John went straight to the pub where he stayed till midnight. When he came home he tried to open the bedroom door but it was still locked. They could hear him in the kitchen talking to himself. Neither said a word for a long while. Finally, Minnie broke the silence. She spoke in a whisper, not wishing her voice to carry.

"Would it not be better to relent a little?" she suggested.

"No." Tom's reply was emphatic.

"But he's acting so queerly."

"You want me to give in to a madman, is that it?"

"No, no, that's not it at all. All I want is for you to make a concession."

"I'll make no concession to drink, woman, and that is that. Now go to sleep."

Minnie Cutler sighed. After a while, she spoke for the last time before falling asleep.

"Who's to say but you're right," she said.

The following evening, Mick Kelly the postman called. He came in his Sunday clothes. The old folk welcomed him. There was no sign of John.

"Sit down, sit down." Tom Cutler pulled a chair from under the table and placed it near the fire.

"And how's herself?" Minnie Cutler asked.

"Never better, missus, thank you," Mick Kelly replied cheerfully.

In any other house in the neighborhood, he would have been royally received. The whiskey bottle would have appeared. The kettle would have been put down to boil. Minnie, who was never embarrassed by similar situations, fumbled for words on this occasion but could find none. Mick Kelly was a good neighbor. For once, she would have liked to offer him something. Her husband read her thoughts.

"I daresay you've had your supper, Mick," he said with forced joviality.

"Just after rising from the table," came the answer.

"You're welcome to eat, you know that," Minnie spoke half-heartedly.

"Oh, I know that, missus," came the reassuring reply, "I know that well."

He made it sound convincing to put Minnie at her ease. He could not recall ever having received as much as a mouthful of tea at Cutler's. Neither could anybody else. Even the beggars of the roadway gave the place a wide berth. Some said there were barely visible scratches on the gate piers down by the main road, the secret sign language of the tinker folk: "Pass by" the scratches said or so it was believed.

For an hour or more the three spoke of weather, crops and cattle, then of the neighbors and lastly of the great wide world. The ancient Stanley range had grown cold for want of fueling. There were a few embers buried in the ashes but to stoke the firebox would be to despatch its entire contents into the ashpan beneath. Mick Kelly knew that it would be unthinkable for the Cutlers to replenish the fire so late in the evening.

"Well," said he and he rose from his chair, "I'll have to be going but before I do I had better bring out what brought me." He cleared his throat and rubbed his large hands together, this to intimate that his mission was a delicate one.

"I've come about John," he said. "You may tell me it's none of my business but I have known the three of you all my life and I feel I have earned the right to bring this matter to your notice." Here he paused, waiting for word to proceed.

"What is it about John?" Tom Cutler asked.

"He's not himself these days," Mick Kelly answered. "He's drinking too much and he's in debt poor fellow. It's not a lot, a few pounds here and there. He owes myself a tenner but that's not why I'm here and I'd gladly forget it if I thought it would help the man."

"Let him stop drinking and he'll soon have his debts paid," Tom cut in.

"I'm afraid," Mick Kelly spoke ruefully, "most of the drink comes from people who are sorry for him."

"He's turned into a bum then, has he?"

"No. That isn't so at all. Most people will throw a drink a fellow's way if they think he has a problem. It's their way of sympathizing."

"What do you want me to do?"

"Raise his wage for a start. Give the poor fellow a few hundred to pay his debts. That's all. I promise you won't know the man after."

"I'll tell you something now, Mick Kelly, and I'll tell you no more." Tom Cutler rose and faced him. He moistened his thin lips before he spoke. "When I took over here there was a crippling debt. I was advised to sell but I stuck it out whatever. It took the best years of my life to pay back the money my father squandered. It was a terrible burden for a young man and now when I'm old you want me to pay my son's debts as well. Is that to be the story of my life, to pay back the debts of two drunkards, my father and my son?"

"I can't counsel you further, Tom," Mick Kelly said quietly. "I can only tell you that all is not well with your son."

"It's not my doing, Mick."

"I didn't say it was, Tom. The poor fellow is demented and what harm but he could have enough if he wanted but he's too bloody honest."

"I don't follow you," Tom Cutler frowned.

"He could be selling the odd bag of corn behind your back and he could be transferring a gallon or two of milk to a crony. There's a lot doing it and getting away with it but not John Cutler. He could be lifting the occasional bag of spuds."

Tom Cutler stamped the concrete floor with his right foot. "He could in his eye," he whipped back. "If there was a grain of corn taken, or a single spud or a solitary pint of milk I'd know about it. He knows that. You know that and I know that and that's the reason he hasn't lifted anything so far. His first time would be his last time. I have another son, remember, a man who wouldn't be long answering my call if I sent for him."

"I beg of you, Tom, not to renege on John." Mick Kelly's appeal was fervent.

"I never reneged on him. He had cattle of his own, remember. He drank the proceeds every time."

"And I tell you he drank no more than anybody else." Mick Kelly stuck to his purpose.

"I'm tired, Mick." Tom Cutler returned to his chair.

He was making it clear that as far as he was concerned the discussion was closed. Mick Kelly looked from husband to wife. For a moment he considered making a final appeal but thought better of it. The eyes of both were now focused on the ashpan of the Stanley. They leaned forward on their chairs the better to gaze upon it. As well as dismissing him, the pose also suggested a show of solidarity.

"Goodnight," Mick Kelly threw back as he opened the kitchen door.

"Goodnight, Mick," they spoke in unison without averting their heads. Mick felt as if he had closed the door on a tomb. He hurried home to his wife. He had promised to tell her how he fared before going to the pub.

As soon as the fall of the year had established itself, John Cutler laid it on the line for the old man.

"I need decking out from head to toes," he said, "and it cannot be put off any longer. You will also double the money you are paying me now. Nothing less will do. Any farmer in the neighborhood would do better by me."

"Let me think about that one for a while," Tom Cutler had told him. "The fall isn't full out yet you know."

It was the way the old man had said it that nettled John. It was as though he had made some outrageously childish claim and had not been taken seriously, had been humorously rebuffed. Was his father playing for time and if so why? The old fellow had been acting too independently of late, not caring whether John rose or slept it out in the mornings, whistling to himself and walking off whenever John grumbled about his lot. It was a totally new and inexplicable phase in their relationship. Had the old man something up his sleeve? John grew moodier as the autumn drew to a close. He was no longer asked to go to the village for farm or household necessities. He suspected he was being subtly isolated. Whenever he entered the kitchen, they busied themselves ostentatiously with needless chores or, if they were engaged in conversation, it was immediately terminated when he put in an appearance. It was as though his father wished him to know that he had better tread warily, that there might be more strings to his bow than were apparent. There could only be one answer.

They had contacted Willie with a view to bringing him home but how to be sure, how to make certain? Mick Kelly would know.

"It's a question I am not at liberty to answer," Mick Kelly told him firmly when John Cutler demanded to know if there had been any exchange of letters between his father and Willie.

"Then there is!" John banged his pint glass triumphantly on the bar counter.

"No," Mick assured him, "there isn't. Take my word for it. You have nothing to worry about from that quarter, at least as far as I know."

John shook his head glumly. "He has some ace in the hole," he said, "it has to be Willie."

The Cutlers did not possess a motor car. The only concession Tom Cutler had made to modernization was to invest in a second-hand tractor and he did this reluctantly. Until the arrival of the tractor he depended on a pair of horses. He greatly deprecated the disposal of these but compensated himself with the purchase of a pony. He refused to buy a motor car. He had a light cart made for the pony and used it to convey himself and Minnie to Mass, for occasional trips to the village and for work in the bog during the turf harvesting. The tractor with a trailer attached was used chiefly for conveying the milk to the village creamery and for general farm work although John used it regularly to get to and from the pub.

As they breakfasted one morning towards the end of September the old man addressed his wife.

"As soon as you've finished the washing-up," he informed her, "I'll tackle the pony for you. There's a few items to be got from the village."

Minnie nodded obediently.

"You'll bring the usual groceries, a quarter pound of three inch nails and eight yards of rope. "'Tis time the turf was drawn out. The laths on the rail need securing and a new reins will be wanted."

Again Minnie nodded dutifully. "Will that be all?" she asked.

"That will be all," Tom Cutler said.

"Bring a handful of fags as well, will you?" John added.

The old couple exchanged looks but no comment was forthcoming. Tom arose and went towards the door. Before going out he turned. "You will bring back the items I ordered," he said, "and no more." Hands in pockets, he went whistling into the sunlight.

Without a word, John rose and followed. His mother would have restrained him but he was gone before she could speak. What she wanted to tell him was that she would bring a few packets of cigarettes unknown to his father but the words just wouldn't come out. She had been frightened by the look on John's face as he left. At first she feared that he would waylay his father and have it out with him but no, he had gone straight to the tractor, started it and driven off. Mick Kelly's words came back to her. "I can't counsel you further," he had said. "I can only tell you that all is not well with your son."

From force of habit she refused to ponder on the problem, concentrating instead on the trip to the village. She sensed, however, that events were coming to a head. Her intuition told her that something would have to be done if a calamity were to be avoided. There was no point in bringing the matter up with her husband. She had tried repeatedly since Mick Kelly's visit but he had smothered every effort at the outset. She resorted to the only means of succor remaining to her. Rummaging in her apron pocket she withdrew her Rosary beads and silently began the long count of Hail Marys. She would pray the whole way to and from the village and she would light candles in the parish church. The thought consoled her. The peace and beauty of the candle altar would be a tonic in itself, the very thing to bring her out of herself. She was unaccustomed to such treats. As she led the pony towards the roadway there was a lightness in her step that she hadn't experienced for months. In the village she saw a tractor which looked like John's outside one of the public houses but her new found elation was such that she felt able to ignore the implications involved. In the church she would find refuge from all embarrassments. There was no doubt in her mind about that and was not this as it should be? Was it not her entitlement?

Mick Kelly dismounted from his motor cycle at the entrance to the Cutler farm. He didn't have a letter but he had resolved to face up to Tom Cutler a second time. The day before, he had encountered Minnie on her way from the village but she had not reined up to talk. Neither had she returned his salute. He had noticed the beads entwined about her fingers. He had remounted then and gone about his business. He had planned a new approach for this second appeal. This time he would draw Minnie into the thick of things whether she wished it or not. He believed that, deep down, she sympathized with John and he would be depending on this. It would be to his advantage if she were alone when he arrived but, failing that, he would involve her anyway. As he neared the house, he sensed there was something wrong, something disproportionate. There was a new and terrible dimension to the area left of the house where the last leaves on a stand of ash trees whispered in the morning wind. There was an ominous addition to the familiar landscape and yet, though he was curious, he could not bring himself to look. This, however, could be that he already knew the awful nature of the intrusion. Slowly he forced his eyes to the left, eyes that started to fill with terror the moment he decided to confirm his worst fears. What he saw before him was the ultimate in physical distortion. The body of John Cutler hung from a stout branch extending from one of the ash trees. Around his neck was the shining new rope his mother had purchased in the village the day before. He was barefoot. His shoes had fallen to the ground. They lay directly beneath his feet. Mick Kelly made the sign of the cross and threw the cycle to one side. His next reaction was to pound the kitchen door. Instead he drew a deep breath and knocked gently. The door was opened at once by Tom Cutler.

"I have bad news." Mick Kelly bent his head to avoid the rheumy eyes. Tom Cutler made his task easy.

"I know," he said, "I was just going for help."

He had, he explained, been changing into a fresh shirt. His shortcoat lay in readiness on the table. Minnie sat soundlessly by the Stanley, her beads clutched in her hands, her body rocking forward and backwards on the chair. All the time her lips moved in prayer.

"Will you take him down?" Tom Cutler asked.

"Yes, of course," Mick answered, surprised by the old man's matter-of-factness. Despite the shock which he must have undergone, he seemed to be his everyday self.

"You'll need a ladder," Tom Cutler said.

"And a knife," Mick enjoined.

"What do you want with a knife?" Tom asked.

"To cut the rope," Mick responded.

"A saw is what you want," Tom reminded him. "A saw to cut the branch."

Mick listened with growing wonder as the old man explained. "A branch can be had for nothing," he said, "a rope costs money. Besides 'tis wanted for a reins."

Buttoning his shortcoat, he led the way to a small out-house. He emerged with a short ladder which he handed to Mick. He re-entered the house and emerged with a rusty saw. He motioned a bemused Mick Kelly to follow him towards the ash grove. Overhead, the dry leaves flickered around his dead son. Some fell to the ground to join the others already rotting there.

Dousie O'Dea

If you were to ask anybody in the parish of Tanvally about Dousie O'Dea the answer would always be the same. She had no equal in the county when it came to the doing up of corpses. As she grew older, she grew selective and practised her art on rare occasions only. Then there came an unhappy day when she announced that she was retiring altogether. Thereafter, nothing could persuade her to continue. She declined even to indulge deathbed wishes.

It was in the little things that Dousie exceled. Where a

wart dominated a certain area of the face when life throbbed in that face's temples there would be no sign in death that a wart ever existed. Hair that in life seemed lank and incapable of curling assumed, under Dousie's coiffeusage, a transfiguration so beauteous that seasoned corpse-viewers could only gasp upon beholding it. She had a special way with wrinkles. As she kneaded the ancient skin of pensioners, these would vanish mysteriously one by one until the texture of the skin on the face of the subject assumed a girlish smoothness. Unsightly pimples were transformed into fetching beauty spots while minor distortions of the neck and ears were so skillfully adapted that they never failed to compliment the visage from which they once detracted.

Once and once only was her handiwork submitted for professional criticism. The cadaver in question was that of one Baldy Mullane, an aged agricultural laborer who suddenly made his farewell to this life while transplanting onions in a plot at the rear of his cottage. Dousie was called upon to ready him for his trip to the next world. This she did without fuss or delay. That night at Baldy Mullane's wake there was porter in abundance. Two half tierces were on tap. Wine and whiskey flowed freely. It had been Baldy's lifelong ambition to be waked decently. At the height of the mourning when the wake-room was crammed with sympathizers, it was announced that an American holidaymaker by the name of Louis Blep had arrived for the dual purpose of paying his respects and inspecting the corpse. Blep was a small, fat, loquacious individual whose mother had been born and reared in Tanvally but was forced to emigrate to the United States in order to find employment. In Chicago she married a successful mortician of German extraction. His name was Ernst Blep. Louis was the sole outcome of the union. Ever since his Confirmation when his mother had first brought him on holiday to her parents' home in Tanvally, Louis had paid regular visits to the maternal homestead. His mother and grandparents were long since dead but there was no scarcity of relations. He would spend a few days with each until his three weeks' holiday expired. Even if he had never heard of Dousie O'Dea's skills as an amateur mortician, his presence would have been expected at the wake-house anyway.

He was greeted on arrival by Baldy Mullane's daughter, Bessie. A brimming glass of whiskey was thrust into his hand. He swallowed it neat at one go. This was the custom. He would be presented with a second glass as soon as he regained his breath after the first. This would be drunk at a more leisurely rate while he sympathized with the relations. As soon as he moved towards the wake-room door, the occupants of the kitchen pressed forward. There were many who wanted to hear him confirm what they had long believed, that Dousie O'Dea was without peer when it came to the doing-up of corpses while others, a minority, hoped only that the visit would be a come-uppance for Dousie. Such is the price of fame and indeed in Tanvally, as in other places, there are always people who are incapable of saying a good word about anybody.

Preparatory to his entry, Louis Blep handed his empty

glass to Bessie Mullane. It would hardly have been in keeping with the occasion had he taken it into the wake-room. Handing it to Bessie was his guarantee that it would be filled upon his return to the kitchen. Louis hesitated for a moment at the wake-room door. He had already resolved to be uncritical of Dousie's efforts. Neither would he over-praise. A pleasant smile and a gentle nod of approval should keep everybody happy. He was quite unprepared for the eye-catching artistry which confronted him from the death bed. Baldy Mullane did not look a day over forty. His head glinted under the light of the sacred candles which stood in their pewter sticks at either side of the bed. The serenity of sanctity shone from his flawless face. If the expression thereon could have been translated into words it would have read: "Gone straight to heaven. Signed Baldy Mullane."

Louis knelt on one knee and whispered a hasty Lord's Prayer for the soul of the deceased. A number of somberly dressed, elderly women sat on sugawn chairs at the other side of the bed. Their trained eyes missed nothing. If Louis Blep's inscrutable features were to register the most insignificant of changes, it would be recorded at once and its character accurately interpreted. From time to time, these frosty-faced fossils exchanged whispers, winks and nudges which spelt approval or disapproval of certain mourners. Otherwise they maintained a stony silence which helped immediately to chasten exuberant or drunken visitors. In fairness to them, they helped to preserve the solemnity of the proceedings. Louis Blep rose and blessed himself, nodded respectfully in the direction of the vigilant elders and vacated the wake-room. A crowd gathered round him. He took momentary refuge in the full glass which Bessie Mullane handed him.

"Well?" A self-appointed spokesman for the group posed the question.

"I seen mugs in my time," Louis Blep, having carefully considered the question, spoke from his heart, "but I ain't never seen no mug like that in there. The guy's positively beautiful. This dame, what's her name?"

"Dousie O'Dea," everybody chorused.

"She's a natcheral. If she was in the States with a talent like that she'd be a millionaire in no time."

This put the seal on Dousie O'Dea's already prestigious reputation. Word of Louis Blep's commendation spread far and wide. From that night forth it was considered sacrilegious when, unwittingly, some innocent spoke disparagingly of Dousie. Her reputation was secure. That was why her retirement came as such a blow to those who had hoped for her ministrations at the end. Years passed but despite constant appeals she steadfastly refused to come out of retirement. As a result, it greatly added to the respectability of a family if they could boast that one of their members had been done up by Dousie O'Dea. It was almost like owning a Stradivarius. It carried with it more esteem than a marble headstone or a Celtic Cross and it wasn't that Dousie had lost her touch or that age had blunted her skill.

In her heart of hearts she knew that all her efforts,

excellent and all as they were, had a sameness, an unchangeable texture, a sort of futile duplication. The cold truth was that no single one stood out above any other. No one would deny that they were all masterpieces and could not be bettered but was this enough? Should not there be one effort which crowned all the others? It was a niggling question and the older she got the more it vexed her. Hard as she tried, she could not recall a particular corpse more pleasing to her than all the others. From her backward vantage point she had no way of knowing that the true artist can never be fully satisfied.

In time, others came to take her place. She frequently viewed the end-products of her imitators. She had no choice. When neighbors died, condolences had to be offered. This meant kneeling by the deathbed for as long as it took to intone a decade of the Rosary. She would have to be blind not to notice the bed's occupant. Always, upon rising, she would pass the same comment: "A handsome corpse God bless her," or if it was a man: "A noble corpse God bless him." She was conceding nothing. Everybody else said exactly the same thing. It was part of the ritual of all wake-house visits. Sometimes when her imitators exceled themselves, the grim-faced custodians of the wake-room would alert themselves for Dousie's reaction. None save the customary comment was ever forthcoming. Then, on a hail-ridden, windy night in mid-January, Dousie O'Dea had unexpected visitors. Her husband Jack it was who answered the timid knocking on the door. Jack and Dousie had not been blessed with issue. For all that, they were well content with themselves and had no great wish for company other than their own.

"Who's out?" Jack O'Dea called.

"'Tis only us," came the response from outside.

"Yes," said Jack O'Dea, "but who is us?"

"Us is Thade and Donal Fizzell."

Jack recognized Thade Fizzell's booming voice.

"I declare to God!" Dousie spoke from her corner of the hearth, "there is nothing so sure as that their sister Jule is dead."

In the doorway the brothers shook the hailstones from their caps and shoulders.

"God bless all here." They spoke in unison.

"Take off the coats and drive on up to the fire," Dousie welcomed them as she rose to take their coats.

"'Tis unmerciful weather entirely," Thade Fizzell spoke to no one in particular.

"A coarse brush I wouldn't put out this night," Donal, the smaller and younger of the pair spoke in support. When all were seated round the fire Dousie took a bottle and glasses from a well-concealed compartment high in the hearth wall. The bottle contained poitcheen. She poured until the brothers protested and then poured an extra dollop in case the protests were token. The brothers were well into their second glasses before conversation began in earnest. It touched first upon the vagaries of the winter weather, then upon the quality of fodder and potatoes until it centered upon the true purpose of the visit. The externals, however, had to be observed regardless of the importance of the news. These outward flourishes helped to emphasize the main item which in this case happened to be, as Dousie had predicted, the recent demise of Jule Fizzell. The brothers were both in their early seventies which meant that Jule who was the oldest of the family could well be eighty years of age.

"Did she go quick, the poor soul?" Dousie enquired after her death had been announced.

"Like that," Thade Fizzell replied and flicked his fingers to indicate the speed of her departure.

"Darning socks she was in front of the fire when the needle tinkled on the hearthstone and the sock fell from her hand."

"May God grant a silver bed in heaven," the aspiration came from Jack O'Dea.

"You know, of course," Thade Fizzell cut short the celestial entreaties, "she was anything but a handsome woman."

The O'Deas nodded sympathetically and waited.

"In fact," Thade continued, "you'd be hard put to find uglier."

"She was," Donal Fizzell subscribed, "the plainest creature I ever came across. I must say in truth, although she was my very own sister, that I used to keep a look-out in my travels for plainer but I looked in vain. Our Jule beat all I ever saw. That woman used to frighten the children on their way home from school. Even the crows avoided our haggard when she cocked her head in the air."

When Donal finished, Thade resumed.

"At dances long ago, men used to talk sideways at the poor creature so as to avoid looking at her direct. In the end, she gave up going to dances and contented herself by her own hearth. Matchmakers came with accounts of likely men but one look was enough for them. What harm but she was as kind-hearted a soul as ever drew breath. There was a great heart cooped inside her breast and I never heard her cast a hard word on any creature living or dead."

Thade Fizzell noted the tears that trickled down Dousie O'Dea's face. He nudged his brother. Donal maintained the advocacy. "That dear soul," he continued, "wanted nothing only to see others happy but she did make one request. Every so often she would say, 'There is something you boys must do for me.' We never had to ask what it was. We knew it well enough from listening day in, day out. 'When I'm stretched on my deathbed you'll bring Dousie O'Dea to do me up.' It wasn't for the Pope of Rome she asked nor cardinals with their red hats. All she wanted was to be done up by Dousie O'Dea."

A long, awkward silence followed. It was Jack O'Dea who broke it.

"Boys," he said, "Dousie is greatly honored by all you say but what you ask is impossible."

"Then let her tell us herself," Thade Fizzell insisted. "We are, at the very least, entitled to that."

"It is as Jack says," Dousie spoke with finality.

"With a face like Jule's," Donal Fizzell said sadly, "there is no hope she'll face for heaven. She'd be too ashamed. She'll most likely linger at the gate forever. I daresay it was too much to ask in the first place for there is no power on earth could transform our eyesore of a sister into a presentable corpse. It just cannot be done."

"I did not say it could not be done," Dousie cut in pertly.

"Then you'll do it?" New hope radiated from Thade's amiable face.

"I didn't say that either," Dousie reminded him, "but, in view of all you have said and taking into account what your poor sister suffered in this world because of her looks, I'll do her up for you but it will be the last time these hands will ever decorate the dead."

The brothers Fizzell could scarcely contain their delight. Old as they were they danced a jig on the flagstone of the hearth but stopped suddenly when Jack O'Dea reminded them that a sister of theirs lay dead. Dousie took immediate charge of the situation as soon as the brothers' rejoicing had fully subsided.

"Jack," she said, "you go straightaway and tackle the cob. You boys go on home and make arrangements for the wake. I'm going to the room for to gather my accoutrements."

At Fizzell's, Dousie worked alone and in silence. She saw to it that the wake-room door was bolted from the inside. She had long determined that her craft, for what it was worth, would go to the grave with her. It had often been suggested that she adopt an apprentice or at least school some of the corpse-dressers who appeared after her retirement in the basics of the business. She had turned a deaf ear to such entreaties. She was well aware that any disclosure on her part would quickly erode the reverence in which she was held. Anyway it was her strongly held contention that corpse-dressers, like poets, were born, not made. Jule Fizzell proved to be the most difficult subject she had ever encountered. Luckily, she had lost none of her old skill. Neither did her long lay-off impede the work in any way. An hour passed and then another. A voice from the kitchen asked if everything was all right. She replied in the affirmative and asked that there be no more such queries. She needed every last iota of her concentration for the job in hand. Indeed there were times when she despaired of effecting any change whatsoever, so complex and craggy were the features under her hands. Perspiration trickled down her face as the night wore on. Yet she persevered until slowly but surely a masterpiece began to take shape. She became a trifle excited as she realized that this might well be the central gem in the wide brooch of her art. In the end, after nearly three hours of sustained effort, she had accomplished the impossible. She sat triumphantly on the bedside of her subject and for the first time in her life savored the heady brew of total artistic satisfaction.

"That's not our sister," were the first words uttered by Donal Fizzell.

Thade simply stood transfixed. After a while, he spoke. "It's our sister all right," he said, "and it's what she might have been like if God had ordained it so."

Jack O'Dea was aware from the moment his eyes met those of his wife that something extraordinary had taken place. When he surveyed the corpse, he felt some of the ecstasy that she had felt. Before him on the bed lay one of the most beautiful women he had ever seen. The face that was once a travesty was now angelic, its sharp contours magically softened by the artistry of his wife. The Fizzell brothers had seated themselves on chairs, their unbelieving eyes firmly fixed on the ravishing creature on the deathbed. Now and then they would shake their heads or exchange mystified looks but no words came. The fact was that there were no words which would do proper justice to Dousie's creation. If there was a word that might be fittingly applied, that word was alive for, in truth, Jule Fizzell had never looked more alive. In life men had looked the other way. In death they would look at Jule Fizzell a second time and remember her haunting beauty long after she had been claimed by the clay. After what seemed like hours, the brothers stirred themselves from the trance which had mesmerized them. There was the wake to think of. The undertaker would have to be approached. Drink would need to be transported from the village. Victuals in plenty would have to be purchased, relatives notified and the hundred and one other items attended to, which all went into the making of a successful wake.

In the parish of Tanvally there are nights which are remembered above all others. There was, for instance, the night of the big wind and the night of Horan's last wrendance. Of like caliber was the night of Jule Fizzell's wake. The mourners came from far and wide. Single, in pairs and in droves they came to view the Fizzell phenomenon.

Those who had known her personally were awestruck by the transformation. Those who came merely out of curiosity were lavish in their praise. None could recall a corpse possessed of so much charm and vivacity. The wake was a success from the outset. Instead of proving to be an embarrassment, as the brothers had feared, their departed sister had brought them honor and glory. They swaggered from kitchen to wake-room accepting sympathy and homage. Midway through the wake, the drink supply ran dangerously low. A courier was quickly despatched to the village where the original order was repeated. It was delivered instantly. The publican in question was requested to be on hand should further supplies be needed. Thade and Donal Fizzell were determined to play their part in making the night a memorable one. Neighbors were commissioned to ensure that no glass remained empty for long. Pots of tea and plates of edibles were in constant circulation. By midnight the house was packed to suffocation. The sole topic of conversation was the corpse. She was showered with superlatives. Hardened reprobates whose previous wake-room contributions rarely exceeded a single, mumbled prayer spent long periods on their knees, their eyes affixed to the deathbed whereon lay the loveliest creature they had ever beheld. There were many who revisited the wake-room several times. These consisted mainly of those who could not at first believe their eyes.

At one o'clock in the morning the drift homewards began. By four, the house was deserted save for Thade and Donal Fizzell and a few cronies who elected to keep them company until daybreak. Having consumed their fill of drink, the entire party lapsed into a drunken sleep around the fire. When they wakened in the morning the corpse had vanished. They looked under the bed but all they found there was a venerable chamber pot which had seen better days. They looked in the other rooms but found no trace of the missing cadaver.

While they had slept a strange thing had happened. In the Tanvally uplands, on a small isolated farm there resided a rough and ready sort of a fellow known far and wide as the Cowboy Cooney. No one knew for sure what his exact age might be. It was certain, however, that he was no chicken. He lived completely alone with neither chick nor child, wife nor parent. His only visitors were poitcheen dealers who came at monthly intervals to purchase his regular output of the precious brew. If, on rare occasions, other callers appeared on the narrow roadway which led to his house, he made himself scarce in the hills and did not return till they had departed. From early afternoon, he had been aware that something of importance had happened in the valley. As night came down and the lights of a hundred transports twinkled on the main road several miles below, he grew alarmed.

"What can it mean?" he asked himself. Had there been an invasion of some kind? Had some unprecedented disaster struck the valley? He withdrew a poitcheen bottle from underneath the thatch and positioned himself on the pier of a gate, the better to view the goings-on in the valley. Lights in their hundreds came and went. With over half the contents of the bottle safely tucked away, the Cowboy decided that the activities down below merited his personal attention. He decided to bring the bottle with him for company. By the time he reached the Fizzell farmhouse which had seemed to him to be the nub of the bustle, he saw only the sleeping figures by the fire. Cautiously he entered and surveyed the scene. On the table standing out from several empty contemporaries was a full bottle of whiskey. Since he had long since emptied his own bottle he put this welcome find to his head and downed at least two glasses in one long, single swallow. It was quite palatable although a lightweight concoction compared to his own home-made drafts. He sensed rather than saw that the cause of all the earlier comings and goings was to be found in the room so romantically flooded by flickering candlelight. He was not prepared for the sight which met his eyes. He stood with his mouth open for several moments utterly overcome by the radiant loveliness of the smiling lady who occupied the bed. It was this very smile which gave him the courage to advance a step or two. The Cowboy Cooney, up until this moment, had always been the very soul of shyness. This was no longer the case. The smile on the face of this wonderful woman on whom he had never before laid eyes had given him poise and confidence. He could see that she wished him to sit on the side of the bed. This he did and at once launched into the story of his life. He wept throughout the tragic aspects and the smile on her face seemed to change to one of sympathy. Emboldened by her obvious fondness for him, he took her hand, not noticing the coldness.

"Will you marry me?" he asked.

At this, she merely smiled but he could see that it was a smile of consent. What a placid, sensitive, modest creature she was.

"Then you'll be mine?" he asked. Again the affirming smile.

"There is no need to speak," he told her, "your smile has spoken for you."

Gently he lifted her into his arms and staggered into the kitchen where he addressed the sleeping inmates.

"I am taking this woman to be my lawful wedded wife," he announced. "If any man here has anything to say, let him speak now or forever hold his peace."

He waited for a reply and was rewarded with an assortment of drunken snores which he took to mean approval. Triumphantly, he blundered into the night. Next morning, they were discovered by a group of schoolchildren. Jule Fizzell was cradled in the arms of Cowboy Cooney. The serene smile on his face was matched only by that on the face of the corpse. He snored blissfully. She made no sound at all.

When, later in the day, the news was relayed to Dousie O'Dea, she smiled to herself. She had reached the final pinnacle. Her life's work was complete. For one man, she had brought the dead to life. For this, in itself, she would be remembered beyond the grave.

The Last Great Hare-Hunt of Ballycoolard

Han Boulter opened the American-stamped envelope and extracted the letter. With great care she unfolded the crisp, almost transparent notepaper to discover three one hundred dollar bills taped to the opening page. Normally, the American letter might contain ten or twenty dollars, even as much as fifty at Christmas but this latest sum was exceptional, although not unprecedented. It could only mean one thing. Her brother, Monsignor Pat, pastor of Saint Sara's parish in Louisville, Kentucky, would be com-

ing home to his native Ballycoolard for an extended holiday in the not-too-distant future. Before addressing herself
to the letter's contents Han Boulter rolled the notes into a
pencil-thick tube and deftly deposited them in the depths
of her ample bosom.

As expected, the letter contained details of the monsignor's proposed itinerary. Alarm gathered on Han's com-
posed features as she calculated the nearness of her
brother's arrival. In less than a week, he would be landing
at Shannon. There was much to be done. The house would
have to be painted inside and out, his room heated, his bed
aired. The neighbors would have to be told. He delighted
in being received on his arrival by all his old friends. Plen-
tiful and varied stocks of drink would have to be laid in.
The monsignor imbibed all kinds. In addition, he was a
gracious and magnanimous host. Often he would sit until
dawn with the friends of his schooldays recalling colorful
incidents from their salad days. Needless to mention, these
excursions into the past required to be fueled by good quality spirits. It would be unthinkable for stocks to run out at
the height of the reminiscing.

Then there was the question of meeting him at the air-
port. That would be the least of her worries, however.
There would be no scarcity of volunteers for this highly-
prized undertaking. The chore, more than likely, would be
allotted by simple right of propinquity to her near neighbor
Danny Doble. Danny had other privileged claims. He was
distantly related to the Boulters and was it not he who was
the monsignor's constant companion when they roved over

the wild uplands of Ballycoolard in childhood days. Anyway wasn't it well known that Monsignor Pat was addicted to Danny's company above all others in the townland. As soon as Han Boulter had thoroughly absorbed every item of relevance in the letter, she immediately launched herself into the drawing up of a comprehensive list of essentials to provide for her brother's stay. After one of these, she erected a large question mark. The item in question was hare-soup. This one-time delicacy was reputed to be the ideal antidote for common or garden hangover. Indeed, as she recalled, Monsignor Pat was more partial to her own particular recipe than to any other broth or brew available locally. He literally lapped it up. The flesh of the hare was never eaten in the countryside. Traditionally, this creature of the wild was associated with the fairy folk. Add to this the fact that the flesh was not particularly gustable or visually attractive and you were nearer the true reason.

Han was well aware that hares were scarce and had been for a number of years. Some blamed modern fertilizers. Others who would not disagree with this altogether put it down to drainage as well. They maintained that the hare's natural and ancient sanctuaries were being transformed into viable grasslands where cover quickly disappeared after grazing or cutting. Still, Han Boulter felt, one solitary hare should not be too hard to come by. She resolved to refer this matter to Danny Doble. For him, it would merely be a labor of love. If there was a hare within a radius of five miles, Danny would discover its whereabouts and see that the animal was executed summarily for soup-making purposes.

When word spread that Monsignor Pat was coming on holiday, there was much rejoicing all over Ballycoolard. After a winter which had truly tested the character of the hill people, the first whispers of the amiable cleric's impending arrival added a special flavor to a newly arrived spring which was little milder than the recent winter. There would be trips to Killarney, to football and hurling matches, regardless of distance. There would be hooleys to which all well-behaved people would need no invitation. The first person to whom Han divulged the sensational news was Danny Doble. She also conveyed her worries about the likelihood of a hare scarcity. He dismissed her fears.

The first thing he did, having advised his cronies about the monsignor's visit, was to arrange a meeting for that very night at the crossroads pub. Here, in front of a blazing turf fire, they discussed ways and means of capturing a hare.

"It would be a terrible thing," Danny Doble told his listeners, "to have no hare after he coming all of that long journey for a drop of hare-soup." Murmurs of approval greeted this pronouncement.

"Time is of the essence," Danny went on. "A hare would need to be hanging three days before he's fit for the pot and we have only six days in all, so here is what I propose. We will appoint a man to reconnoiter Ballycoolard from top to bottom, from one end to the other. He will set out tomorrow morning and report back here to us tomorrow night. We will then prepare ourselves for the greatest hare hunt ever to be carried out in this part of the world. We will begin after first Mass on Sunday morning."

Cries of "hear-hear" and other expressions of approval were readily forthcoming. Only one question remained to be resolved. Who would be chosen for the task of inspecting the countryside? Names were mentioned but their proprietors were either too young or too old, too short-sighted or too near-sighted. In the end, the name of Bronc Muldoon was mentioned most. He had earned his nickname the hard way. A bare-back rider of asses, ponies and mules from the moment he could walk, he had fallen off many times, nearly always upon his head. This had left him permanently confused, a sort of child of the wilds who was closer to nature than any living person in Ballycoolard. There was no questioning his stamina or speed. Out of the way places in hill and dale were his favorite haunts. He was young and he was eager. Most important, he was fitted for little else.

The instructions given him were that he was to scour the region until he sighted a hare or any number of hares. Under no circumstances was he to disturb or molest the creatures. Most hares lope indolently around a chosen area or rest in their secluded forms unless agitated by hounds or fowlers. For the most part they tend to ignore disinterested humans so that the Bronc's intrusion into hare country was not likely to provoke any dramatic departure from one area to another.

"Make your sighting and proceed about your business

until you have the whole of Ballycoolard covered," was the advice tendered by Danny Doble. The elders in the company recalled likely hare habitats while the Bronc assiduously repeated all he was told in a loud voice. A rough map of the district was drawn up by the school-master. On it a starting place was prominently marked and, from this point, a heavy red line ran circuitously through the prescribed terrain until the ultimate boundary was reached. Then, and not till then, was the Bronc to return home. It was expected that he would encounter more than one hare and more than one group of hares provided his search was industrious and comprehensive.

"In the event of this happening," Danny Doble warned, "you will make immediate recourse to your map and mark your sightings conspicuously."

"Yes," the schoolmaster put in, "and in so doing you will provide us with the blueprint of our hunt and spare us much time and labor on Sunday."

The group stayed on in the pub after closing time, recalling to mind memorable hunts and doughty hares which once extended them beyond the limits of their endurance. The following morning, the Bronc Muldoon was up at first light. His widowed mother, aware of the importance of the task ahead of him, provided him with a breakfast fit for a ploughman. The Bronc, as was his wont, left not a single morsel on the place. While he was eating, she packed a substantial lunch. This together with a quart bottle of milk she placed in an ancient haversack which had seen better days. Her last act was to douse him liberally with holy water.

The first thing the Bronc did after he left the house was to eat the lunch his mother had prepared for him. He then sought and discovered a shady, dry shelter where he slept for a few hours. When he awoke, his conscience got the better of him. Without further ado, he made a hasty study of the map and proceeded to the starting point. Darkness had fallen by the time he reached the pub at the crossroads. A large crowd had foregathered. Around the open hearth fire were seated the elders and men of stature such as the schoolmaster and Danny Doble. Breathlessly, the Bronc recounted all he had seen. He made no mention whatsoever of hares until pressed by his listeners to do so.

"I never in all my born days," said the Bronc, "seen so many hares in the same place at the same time."

"Where exactly was this?" Danny Doble asked.

"At the end of Jackeen Quinlan's cutaway," the Bronc promptly replied. At the same time, he produced the map where he had marked the exact spot, as instructed.

"You say you never saw so many hares?" Danny Doble sought confirmation of the Bronc's announcement.

"Never saw so many," the Bronc told him, "but for I watching my step," he continued, "I would have been standing down on the devils." For the remainder of the night he was handsomely plied with porter. Towards closing time he was inclined to ramble but no one was perturbed by this. The map was in the safe keeping of the schoolmaster and that was all that mattered. Plans were carefully laid for Sunday's hunt. It was decided that the force would split up into two parties and arrive at the location from two opposite approaches. This would reduce the chances of the hares escaping.

At early Mass on Sunday, Father Morrigan, the parish priest, gave his blessing to the hunt and, immediately afterwards, Danny Doble reviewed the entire party in front of the church. It consisted of thirty-seven men and boys, three good-class coursing grayhounds and two score other dogs of every conceivable breed and size. Rain fell heavily from the outset, obscuring surrounding fields and bogland but failing to dampen the spirits of the hunters. At the crossroads pub, the party divided itself in two. The schoolmaster was the unanimous choice to lead one half while none contested Danny Doble's right to command the other. Ahead went the dogs and beaters while the rest followed in high spirits. Quickly the miles fell behind but no hare was encountered. This was to be expected. In his reconnaissance of the day before, the Bronc Muldoon had discovered no hare until he reached Jackeen Quinlan's cutaway. It was now more apparent than ever that they were on the right track. All the time the rain fell mercilessly but not a whisper of complaint was to be heard from human or hound. Some of the party who had not anticipated the continuing downpour were drenched to the skin. If anything this made them more resolute. Rivulets of rainwater ran downward from foreheads to chins whence they seeped under shirt collars and scarves. The dogs were silent now. They still panted hopefully, ears ever ready to prick at the sight of game, egged on by their handlers whenever they snapped at each other or dawdled to sniff at imaginary spoors. The handlers were otherwise silent as were the rest of the hunters. Above the labored breathing of the older members of the band was to be heard the juicy squelching of rain-sodden footwear. Still they proceeded at a sapping pace until shortly before noon the Doble contingent found itself confronted by the vast expanse of Jackeen Quinlan's cutaway. There was, as yet, no indication that the second party had arrived. They waited silently for the pre-arranged signal. This was to consist of two blasts, one long and one short, on a referee's whistle. Danny Doble's keen eyes swept the cutaway for signs of life. He expected none for the cover was intense but there was always the outside possibility that a young hare would be panicked into breaking at the unexpected blasts of the whistle. The cutaway covered an expanse of fifty or so acres. It abounded in heavy snipe grass. Yard by yard they worked themselves towards their approaching comrades.

"Any second now," Danny Doble called out, "any second now they'll break. Be ready." The dogs, sensing the orgy of slaughter, set up a deafening outcry. Eventually, both parties met in the center of the cutaway. Most were fit to collapse after the daunting foray through the snipe grass. "Where are all the hares?"

The words were spoken by the youngest member of the gathering. Nobody was prepared to answer his question. The older members looked about them in disbelief and then at each other in perplexity. The same outspoken question was written on every rain-washed face.

"Where are the hares?" Angry mutterings followed. Then came the most pertinent question of all. "Where was the Bronc Muldoon?" As the party consulted with the Bronc's neighbors it transpired that he had not taken part in the hunt. He had, in fact, not been seen at all that morning. Nobody had called for him. All had presumed that, because he was an integral part of the hunt, he would automatically be present. The party returned to their respective homes in a despondent state. They had failed miserably in their task. All they had to show for the day's outing were soggy clothes down to the very undergarments and running noses which were surely the harbingers of heavy colds and aching joints. There was not a man or boy in Ballycoolard who didn't heartily curse the Bronc Muldoon that night.

Inevitably, the blame for the entire debacle, having flitted from one eminent member of the hunt to another, attached itself to Danny Doble. It was he, after all, who organized the expedition into Jackeen Quinlan's cutaway. Nobody said so to his face but he sensed the disillusionment when he visited the crossroads pub the night after the hunt. There was no outright hostility nor was there the slightest dispraise for the way he had handled things. He was wise enough to keep his mouth firmly shut regarding the events of the day before, lest he provoke spoken disapproval. Oddly enough, nobody blamed the Bronc.

"Not the full shilling," was the worst that was said about him. Danny, however, was adamant that the blame should find its proper resting place. Shortly before closing time, the Bronc put in his customary appearance.

"What'll you have?" Danny Doble asked. The Bronc, although suspicious of the offer, intimated that he would not be opposed to a pint of stout. Danny permitted him a first swallow before standing him with his back to the open fire in full view of everybody.

"Tell us now," said Danny in a pleasant voice, "exactly how many hares you saw in Jackeen Quinlan's cutaway?"

A hush fell on the company. The Bronc made no attempt to answer. Danny repeated the question, this time in a more demanding tone. The Bronc swallowed hard and moistened his lips. He looked from face to face but nowhere was there sympathy to be found. Neither was there condemnation.

"Twelve hares was what I saw all told," he blurted out.

"How many?" Danny asked in his most challenging tone.

"Six," from the Bronc.

"How many?" Danny had him on the run and knew it. He pressed home his advantage. "Come on, Bronc. How many?"

"Three." The Bronc bent his head rather than look his accuser in the eye.

"For the last time, Bronc," Danny was adamant now, "how many hares did you see?"

Bronc made no verbal reply. He lifted the index finger of his left hand to indicate that one hare was all he had seen. The gesture failed to satisfy Danny Doble.

"Are you prepared to swear on your solemn oath that

it was a hare you saw?"

Hangdog now, the Bronc made no attempt to answer. He looked for an avenue of escape but there was none.

"What exactly did you see in Jackeen Quinlan's cutaway?" Danny asked after a while. The Bronc muttered an inaudible response.

"Louder," came the relentless prompting of his interrogator.

"What I saw," the Bronc blurted out the words, "was Jackeen Quinlan's cat and not a hare."

"Not a hare? And not three nor six nor twelve hares?" Danny persisted with the inquisition.

"Not three nor six nor twelve hares," the Bronc replied.

"Only Jackeen Quinlan's cat?" Danny rose unsteadily as he launched the final poser. With the aplomb of a truly accomplished advocate, he waited for the Bronc's confirmation.

"Only Jackeen Quinlan's cat," the Bronc whispered.

Danny Doble bowed to left and right as if to judge and jury, finished his whiskey and sauntered with his hands entwined behind his back into the starry world outside.

Protocol

I could tell from the expression on Timmy Binn's face that he had come down from the hilltop on a special mission. Most times he called merely to pass away the winter nights. He would sit by the hearth with my uncle and his wife and maybe her father if the old man felt up to it. There they would exchange news and views until midnight when the party broke up after a cup or two of tea.

My uncle's house sat snugly in the lee of a small Sitka spruce plantation at the bottom of the hill whereas the

Binn abode was almost at the top about a mile distant. At the time, Timmy Binn was approaching his seventieth year which made him the youngest of three bachelor brothers and three spinster sisters who lived together in their ancient farmhouse which looked down on every other in the parish.

The isolation suited the Binns. They were seen in public by early morning massgoers only. These, for the most part, would be old and retiring like themselves, venturing forth weekly to the village church in order to observe the Sabbath.

Timmy it was who did all the shopping. Every morning, Sunday included, he tackled the old black mare to the milk cart and guided her to the creamery with the tanks containing the daily yield from the twelve milch cows. When the milk was delivered, he would purchase the necessary provisions and return home without further delay.

On Fridays, he collected the several old age pensions due to his brothers and sisters at the village post office. Half of the money was spent on luxuries like coil tobacco, snuff and mixed fruit jam. The other half was credited to a joint account in a well-worn post office book. This was left untouched over the years so that it might meet wake and funeral expenses when, one by one, the Binns would be faced with the ultimate contingency.

"Come up to the fire," my uncle called as soon as the door was closed.

Timmy's mouth opened to say something but he thought better of it and sat by the fire as instructed.

"You'll take a bottle of porter," the uncle said. "In fact," said he before Timmy could answer, "we'll all take a bottle of porter."

Normally Timmy Binn would have been offered tea but Christmas was not long past and there still remained some bottled porter after the festivities. The uncle uncorked three bottles. He handed one to Timmy and another to his father-in-law. The third he kept for himself. No glasses were used.

"Sláinte," said the uncle, as he lifted the bottle to his mouth.

"Sláinte," the others answered and they did likewise.

Each went halfway down and as soon as Timmy Binn had placed his on the floor at the side of his chair he readied himself to make an announcement. None came however. From where I sat reading at the kitchen table, I could see that he was under great strain. He wanted to come out with something but couldn't. I was about to intervene and say "Let Timmy talk," but I remembered that it was the custom to exhaust every other topic before asking for the reason behind any visit. I remembered that Timmy had arrived only a few weeks before on an errand for his sisters. He had spent nearly two hours talking in front of the hearth with my uncle and the old man. Finally, when he was handed a cup of tea by the woman of the house, he announced that he would not have time to drink it. He explained that he had been sitting in his own kitchen while his sisters were preparing supper when they suddenly discovered that there wasn't a grain of sugar in the house. Timmy had been dispatched straightaway for the loan of a cupful till morning. He nevertheless allowed himself to be coerced into drinking the tea on the grounds that his sisters would have gone ahead with the supper anyway in view of his long absence.

This time, however, an uncharacteristic agitation showed. He fussed and fidgeted but restrained himself, remembering that there was a ritual to be observed. Neither my uncle nor the old man commented on his restlessness. They presumed that he would withhold the reason for his visit as a matter of course until such time as he was asked. They knew quite well that he had come for a purpose other than sitting and talking but part of the proceedings consisted of endeavoring to deduce in their own minds precisely what that purpose was. The whole undertaking would be spoiled if he came out with his business straight-off. It mattered not how pressing that business might be nor did it count that he might be in a hurry back home. Tradition obliged him to sit it out until the proper time.

"There are poor people sheltering this night without a fire."

The old man of the house swallowed the remainder of his stout after he had spoken. He handed the empty bottle to my uncle in such a manner as to suggest that the opening of three more bottles might not be inappropriate.

"A good blaze is everything," his daughter said, lovingly laying three large black sods on the perimeter of the fire, "and I'll tell you what is more," she went on, "a good fire will draw pain out of a body."

"Tuck, tuck," her father said in agreement.

The uncapped bottles were handed out again and the menfolk quaffed. A lengthy silence followed during which Timmy Binn stirred uneasily in his chair. My uncle and the old man exchanged knowing glances.

"We're on a big one this time," the old man's expression spoke for him.

"No doubt about that," my uncle's said.

The silence continued. They were searching for clues, putting together bits and pieces of information from the happenings of the previous weeks. Something out of the ordinary had happened at Binn's, something not quite calamitous but yet important enough to make an easygoing hillman like Timmy Binn uneasy and fidgety.

"I mind worse winters nor this," the old man spoke to relieve the tension.

"Tell us about the time of the big snow," his daughter urged.

"I was only a boy then," the old man began.

We had heard the story twenty times but it was well suited to a winter's night and it always improved in the retelling. Even Timmy Binn seemed to forget his assignment as the tale unfolded. All the while, the wind howled in the chimney and now and then a shower of passing hailstones beat furiously on the windows. The narrative ended after a half hour with the old man declaring that he needed a drop of something stronger than common porter to restore his flagging energy.

"Storytelling is dry work." This was a favorite saying of his. Without a word, his daughter removed herself and returned a moment later with a bottle of whiskey.

"I was keeping it for an occasion," she explained, "but I suppose this is as good an occasion as any."

She too sensed that Timmy was the bearer of exceptional tidings. The whiskey was her contribution to the prolongment. A woman less sensitive to the lifestyle of the countryside might have terminated the program there and then by simply doing nothing.

"Any sign of snow up your way, Timmy?" The uncle tendered the spirits and the question at the same time.

"The odd flake is all I've seen so far," Timmy answered.

"The odd flake, eh?" The old man pondered the response as he searched for further questions in his whiskey glass. Failing to find any, he lifted it to his lips and skillfully tossed a dollop into his mouth where he allowed it to remain for a while before swallowing it with great relish. It provided him with the inspiration he needed. He was activated by an almost imperceptible spasm as the whiskey reached its destination. He nodded appreciatively.

"Right on target," he said to nobody in particular. "If the first shot hits the bullseye," he declared, "then all the other shots will do the same. It is vital, therefore, to hold the whiskey under your tongue until the stomach is ready to receive it. People don't know how to drink whiskey anymore. Nowadays they swallow it back like it was water and they're paralysed drunk before they know it."

For a quarter hour, he held forth on the subject of whiskey drinking. Whether it was the porter or the whiskey or both, Timmy Binn had more or less resigned himself to the situation. He looked blankly into the fire as the old man roamed aimlessly over a wide field of topics. The uncle took over just as it seemed his father-in-law must topple into sleep from sheer verbal exhaustion. The uncle lacked the narrative skills of the old man but he, nevertheless, managed to contain the visitor with the sheer forcefulness of his dialog. All the while, the old man nodded drowsily but yet managed to stay awake. His daughter sat nearer to him so as to act as a prop whenever he leaned sideways. The uncle supported him on the other side.

Silently I went out of doors. The hail had stopped. The roadway had a bleached look. On the hilltop the Binn farmhouse was ablaze with light. I half expected to see one of the brothers descending the narrow roadway in search of Timmy but the hill road was empty. Undoubtedly there was something amiss at the top of the hill. Up until this time there had been but a single faint light to indicate the whereabouts of the Binn habitation. Now there was this unprecedented radiance shimmering outrageously in the lofty distance like a newly transfixed star of great magnitude. It outshone every other light in the countryside. Then a fleeting cloud obscured the moon and total darkness fell on the roadway. I hurried back to the house. Before going in, I looked through the window into the kitchen. The old man's head dropped as he sat squeezed upright by his daughter and the uncle. She occupied herself with the darning of a sock, nodding in assent at the observations being made by her husband. For his part, he sat with flushed face and held forth for all he was worth using his long arms to stress the elements of his narrative that needed stressing. His mouth opened and closed with great rapidity. It seemed a grim tale indeed but it had little effect on the visitor.

Timmy Binn sat with his legs outstretched, his head forward on his chest as though he had been hypnotized, his empty glass cupped loosely in his grimy hand looking as if it must fall to the floor at any moment. Then the uncle suddenly finished his talk and twiddled his thumbs.

"What's the night like outside?" He asked the question as soon as I had re-occupied my chair.

"Black as pitch," I answered.

"You won't get blacker than that." This affirmation was addressed to Timmy Binn who emerged slowly out of his trance.

"What was that?" he asked apologetically.

"It don't matter," the uncle reassured him.

"Anyone on the road?" the woman of the house asked.

"Not a living Christian," I answered, "except that there is a fierce light on the hilltop."

The lethargy which held sway for so long suddenly disappeared. Everybody was attentive.

"What part of the hill?" the uncle asked.

"Where Binn's is," I answered, as casually as I could.

"Where Binn's is?" It was the old man coming into his own once more. This was the moment for which Timmy Binn had waited all night. Every eye was now turned upon him. His time had come at long last. A total of two and a half hours had passed since he first set foot in the kitchen. He placed his glass on the floor between his legs and folded his hands over his stomach, waiting for the question that was to be his cue. It was posed by the old man.

"And pray, Timmy," he said innocently, "what business brought you down from the hill this night?"

"I would be wanting the loan of six or eight chairs," said Timmy Binn.

"Why would you be wanting six or eight chairs?" It was the uncle's turn now.

"Because," said Timmy Binn, "one of us is dead and we're short of chairs for the wake."

A brief silence ensued during which the uncle and the old man exchanged I-told-you-so glances. They had guessed right. They had been on a big one. The wait had been worthwhile and despite the importance of the mission due protocol had been observed. That was what really mattered.

"You're on Next Sunday"

You'll find more than a few to tell you that there isn't a word of truth in the following story and the nearer you come to the place where it happened you'll find a lot more. When I taxed the man who told me the story with these facts, he took his pipe from his mouth, spat into the fire and looked me between the eyes for an embarrassingly long spell. He did not speak but, when he returned the pipe to his mouth, I knew that the tale was true and that those who belied it were either knaves or fools.

It happened on the fifteenth day of August in the year of our Lord, as they say in these parts, 1934. It was a fair year for primroses, a better one for hay and a woeful year for funerals.

"The Fifteenth" as it is still called locally is the annual Pattern Day in the lovely seaside resort of Ballybunion. From all quarters of Kerry, Cork and Limerick would come thousands of country people in every mode of conveyance from bike to omnibus to shanks' mare and pony cart. They still come but in nothing like the vast numbers of yore.

That particular Fifteenth, as I recall, broke fair and clear. Skies were blue. The air was fresh and wholesome and there was a hearty trace of fine breeze from the west. At the creameries and dispensaries that morning, man, woman and child wore happy faces.

"'Tis a great day for the Fifteenth," they would say to each other and back would come the reply, "ah sure, 'tis a great day entirely." At quarter to eleven in the noon of the day, my grand-uncle Morrisheen Digley went forth to the haggard to catch the pony and, at the turn of the noon, he set forth for Ballybunion in his newly varnished trap. It would do your heart good to see the dancing legs of the pony and the squinting sparks on the flinty road when his iron-shod hooves made light of the long haul. I did not go on the occasion. He said I was too young. Instead he called for his old crony Thady Dowd of Lacca. Neither of the two was under seventy but none gamer set out that day for Ballybunion.

They untackled the pony in the back yard of Mikey

Joe's Irish-American Bar and celebrated their arrival at the Pattern with two glasses of potstill whiskey. This was followed by a brace of pints, pints of creamy black porter. These were consumed so that the remains of the whiskey might be entirely scoured from the gullet, a most advisable practice this if one is to believe those who are fond of indulging in such procedural drinking.

Towards evening they walked as far as the beach to savor the salt sea air and to partake of a paddle near the shore. According to the old people there was nothing the equal of a paddle in the salt water to cure what might be wrong with you. It was pleasant on the shore. The fresh Atlantic breeze was sharp and bracing but as yet without its late autumnal sting. There were hundreds like themselves pacing up and down, ankle deep in the water, content to dawdle aimlessly until the anxiety for drink returned.

In the village, they met neighbors from the townland of Lacca and between them they started a singsong in one of the public houses. When darkness fell, a great hunger for meat seized them. They repaired to a café where they were served with succulent steaks and roast potatoes. This was followed by two dishes of rich trifle and the lot was washed down by several cups of strong, well-sugared tea.

"This will make a handy base for more drink," my grand-uncle announced to Thady Dowd. Dowd nodded agreement happily. So far the pair had enjoyed themselves thoroughly and the night was still but a starry-eyed child in swaddling clothes. The best was to come. After the meal they embarked on a grand tour of the village pubs and had a drink in every one.

At this stage, the reader will begin to raise an eyebrow or two and wonder what is the purpose in the retelling of such a commonplace narrative. Was not their visit to the Pattern but a replica of other years, a common jaunt indulged in by thousands of others and all following the same predictable course?

Patience, dear reader, and bear with me. As soon as the time came to close the pubs three pairs of well-made civic guards appeared on the street and by their presence ensured that every tavern was cleared. The publicans were grateful enough for theirs had been a long and arduous day. By this stage, Thady Dowd and my granduncle had more than their share of strong drink but, for the purpose of shortening the road home, they invested in a half pint of whiskey apiece at Mikey Joe's American Bar.

Earlier, they had plied the pony with a sufficiency of oats and when they came to tackle him they found him in excellent fettle. Like all animals who have spent a long day away from the green pastures of home, he was full of taspy for the task before him. As soon as he found the open road free from obstacles he started to trot in real earnest. Overhead, a full moon lit up the countryside and the sky, its full complement of stars visible in all its quarters, shone like a treasure-house. In the body of the trap the semi-drunken companions sang at the top of their voices to the steady accompaniment of the pony's clopping hooves.

They sang song after song and from time to time they

would uncork their whiskey bottles and partake of whole-some slugs. This made them sing all the louder and soon every dog in the countryside was responding. There was an unholy cacophony as the miles fell behind them.

Then, suddenly, for no reason whatsoever, the pony stopped in his tracks and, despite their most earnest entreaties, would not be coaxed into moving a single, soli-tary inch.

"What's the matter with the creature anyway?" Thady Dowd asked indignantly.

"Beats me," said my granduncle.

All around there was an unearthly silence save for the chuckling of the Gale River which lay just ahead of them, spanned by a narrow bridge. It was the same Gale that poor Spenser the poet did not forget when he wrote about Irish rivers. On the left the crosses and tombstones of Gale churchyard stood pale and gray in the drenching moon-light. The pony stood rooted to the roadway, head bent, his whole frame taut and tense. There was white foam at the corners of his mouth and a look of abject terror, terrible to behold, in his bloodshot eyes.

"I don't like the look of things," my granduncle whis-pered.

"A rattling damn I don't give," Dowd shouted, "I'm get-ting out of here to see what the matter is."

"Stay as you are," my granduncle counseled but there was no stopping the headstrong Dowd. He jumped on to the roadway and walked round trap and pony several times.

"There's nothing here," he called out. He then proceeded towards the river thinking that some calamity might have overtaken the bridge and that the pony, with its animal instinct, might have sensed this. The bridge was in perfect order. Dowd looked over its twin parapets into the shallow, warbling water. He could see nothing unusual.

He retraced his steps and with a scornful toss of his gray head went towards the graveyard of Gale. As soon as he entered the little byroad which led to the gateway, the pony lifted its head and followed slowly. It is well to remember that at no time did my granduncle leave the trap. He sat stiffly, holding the reins, carefully following his friend's every move.

When Dowd leaned across the gate of the graveyard he emitted a loud yell of genuine surprise. There before him were two hurling teams dressed in togs, jerseys and slippers. Every hurler had a hurley in his hand and at one side sitting on a low tombstone sat a small inoffensive-looking, bald-headed man. He wore a white jersey as distinct from the two teams who wore red and green respectively. He had a sliotar or hurley ball in one hand and in the other he held an ancient, burnished, copper hunting horn.

The pony had stopped dead a second time opposite the gateway over which Dowd was leaning.

"Come away out of that," my granduncle called out, "and leave the dead to themselves."

"What's the use?" Dowd called back, "the pony won't budge till it suits these people."

"What's the matter?" he called out to the hurlers who

stood about as if they were waiting for something special to happen. At first no one heeded him but when he called out belligerently a second time a tall player with a face the color of limestone approached the gate. He explained to Dowd that he was the captain of the red-jerseyed hurlers but that the game could not start because his team was short a man.

"Who are these teams anyway?" Dowd asked cheekily.

The captain explained that his team was Ballyduff and the other team Ballybawn.

"Ho-ho," cried Dowd exultantly. "I'm your man. My mother, God be good to her, was a Ballyduff woman. If you have no objection, I will play with your team."

The captain nodded silently and, when my granduncle called to Dowd to abandon his arrant foolishness, the captain turned and addressed him where he sat in the trap.

"Not an inch will you or your pony move," said he in a hollow, haunted voice, "until the final horn is sounded in this game of hurling."

My granduncle said no more. The pony stood now like a statue and the sounds of the river were no longer to be heard. Overhead the moon shone brightly and the pitch which was the length and breadth of the graveyard, was illuminated as though it were floodlit. Forms appeared from the ground and sat themselves on the graveyard wall. The referee looked upwards at the moon and after a few moments' wait blew upon the hunting horn. Then he threw in the ball.

The exchanges started slowly enough with Dowd's

team, Ballyduff, getting the worst of it from a faster Bally-bawn side. The first score came when the referee awarded a free puck to Ballybawn. He also cautioned a number of the Ballyduff players, notably Dowd and the captain, for abusive language towards himself and for dirty play in general.

The Ballybawn skipper drove the ball straight between the uprights. On the graveyard walls, the partisans went wild and a fist fight broke out near the gate. Somebody flung an empty cocoa canister at the referee and he threatened to call off the game if the crowd did not behave themselves. There were a number of fistic exchanges on the field of play but, by and large, the standard of hurling was as good as my granduncle had seen for many a day. There were many fluent movements and excellent long-range scores. The wrist work and pulling left little to be desired. Half time came and went and now the two teams were playing for all they were worth. Time was slipping away and, with five minutes to go, the sides were level.

Neither would yield an inch. Every player strove man-fully to register the single score that would put his own team ahead of the other. The ghostly forms jumped up and down on the walls, egging the players on to greater deeds.

It seemed as if the game must end in a draw and the granduncle noted that, from time to time, the referee looked nervously at the full moon and feverishly fingered his hunting horn, anxious for full time to roll round so that he might wash his hands of the whole affair. There is nothing a referee loves so dearly as a drawn game. The hopes of both sides are kept alive and it is unlikely that he will be assaulted as he leaves the pitch. With less than a minute remaining, there was a mêlée at midfield in which Dowd was involved. Fists flew and hurleys were raised. More than once could be heard the clash of ash against doughty skulls.

The referee intervened and, taking a scroll from his togs' pocket, he commenced the business of taking names. It was during this lull that Dowd sat on a convenient tombstone to savor a richly-merited breather. He withdrew the half-pint bottle from his trousers pocket and dolefully surveyed the remnants of his whiskey. The bottle was still quarter full. He raised it to his lips and, without once taking it from his head, swallowed the contents. Almost immediately, he heaved a great sigh which could be heard all over the graveyard. Then he tightened his trousers' belt and waited for play to resume.

With seconds remaining, the hunting horn was sounded yet again and the ball was thrown in. Dowd it was who won possession. With a fierce and drunken yell, he cut through his opponents like a scythe through switchgrass with the ball poised on the base of his hurley. There were times when he darted like a trout and times when he bounded like a stag. He leaped over grave mounds and skirted crosses and tombstones at breakneck speed. All the time, he edged his way nearer the opposing goal line.

Seeing an opening on the left wing, he seized his chance and headed straight for the goal with the entire Ballybawn team on his heels like a pack of hungry hounds.

Thirty yards out, he stopped dead and took a shot. The ball went away to the right but, if it did, it passed through the eye of a Celtic cross and rebounded off the head of a plaster angel. The rebound was deflected towards the goal by the extended hand of the figure of Michael the Archangel. It skeeved the left upright and found its way to the back of the net.

Need I mention that while the ball was traveling, so was the empty whiskey bottle which Dowd, with sound foresight, had flung at the Ballybawn goalkeeper as soon as the referee's back was turned. The crowd went wild. The Ballyduff team and supporters milled around Dowd and embraced him. Then they lifted him aloft and trotted round the graveyard on a lap of victory. Finishing the lap, the Ballyduff captain called for three cheers for their visitor. Three eerie ullagones went heavenwards and died slowly till the muted river sounds took over once more. The teams had suddenly vanished save for the tall, ghostly presence of the Ballyduff captain. For the first time in over an hour, the pony stirred. He pawed the dirt boreen, anxious for the high road.

"Come on at once," my granduncle called. Dowd, escorted by the captain, made his way towards the gate where the pony was now prancing and difficult to restrain. Dowd shook hands with the captain and was about to depart when a ghostly hand was laid firmly on his right shoulder. The captain leaned forward and whispered into Dowd's ear. Whatever it was he said, Dowd's face underwent a terrible change. The glowing red nose was now puce-colored and the rosy, whiskey-tinted cheeks were ashen gray. Slowly, almost painfully, he climbed across the gate while the captain faded like a breeze-driven mist behind him.

In the trap Dowd was silent and thoughtful. On his face was a woebegone look that struck a chill in my granduncle's heart. The pony highstepped his way homewards, his dark mane flowing loosely behind him, his firm rump bobbing up and down as the miles passed by.

Finally my granduncle popped the question.

"What in heaven's name did he say to you?" he asked.

Dowd shook his head sadly before he replied. Then he spoke slowly and deliberately with a crack in his voice.

"He informed me," Dowd announced, "that because of the way I played tonight I would be on for good next Sunday."

The Fort Field

Grass for ten cows and water for a million!" The old man laughed when he said it.

It was a long time ago. We were driving the cows down the bohareen for the evening milking. We were in a hurry. There was to be a football game that evening in Castleisland. A Tralee team was coming and there was talk of a needle. Through the yellow whins that stood out against the green hedges I could see his small fields, some still glinting sogginess in the height of summer.

"There's a play here," I told myself. The old man is the hero and his wife is the heroine. The ten cows and the other livestock are the characters, all but one. I am the chorus. You notice I leave the villain till last. Yet he was there from the very beginning. He is the water, the ever-present, the everlasting, the accursed water.

The old man used to boast good-humoredly in public houses that a man on horseback could not ride round the whole of his farm in a day. Strangers would shake their heads in incredulity but those who knew his terrain would wait patiently for the explanatory foot note.

"'Tis true for me," the old man would say. "Horse and rider would be drowned after the Fort Field."

As we neared the whitewashed cow-stall, next to the dwelling-house at the little road's end, we leaned over the five-bar gate to look into this field. It was a special place with a character of its own, snug as a carpeted parlor with a green more vivid than any of its neighbors. It was covered with good quality clover and natural vetches, the kind of field the man above makes especially to compensate for all the other squelchy, boggy acres. In spite of the fact that it was surrounded by inferior pastures, it yet managed to remain aloof. It was similar in appearance to the excellent land one sees through a train window as one nears Dublin and I often asked myself what it was doing in the middle of total strangers.

It was so-called because of an ancient redan which occupied its furthest corner with its apex facing towards the gate. There were many such archaic redoubts in the district, but none had the purpose or individuality of this particular one.

The field comprised one acre, one rood and thirty-two perches. Needless to mention, it was pampered. It was conceded more cartloads of dung than any of the others and it was well-supported with annual investments of lime. Nothing was too good for it. It was the best-drained on the whole farm and I suspect it was a showpiece.

In spite of our hurry, we lingered at the gate. I knew he would make no move until I spoke. I knew what was expected of me. I climbed onto one of the concrete piers and donned my admiration look.

"That's a powerful parcel of land," I said, after a little while.

To this he made no reply, but, from his even breathing, I knew I had registered.

"'Tis as fine a bit of land," I went on, "as you'd find if you footed it from Portmagee to Tarbert Island."

He patted a passing cow on the rump but said nothing. This was to show how modest he was. He always pretended he didn't care.

"It's a field," I said, "fit for a racehorse."

He spoke then, for the first time.

"'Tisn't bad," he admitted. "'Tisn't the worst anyhow."

For a man who was supposed to be in a hurry, he showed little inclination towards getting a move on. I knew I had better bring things to a close; otherwise we might miss the football game. I had to end on the highest possible note and so I racked my brain for a conclusive compliment. He was expecting it. He tapped one foot impatiently.

"'Tis a land worth fighting for," I said suddenly, remembering the phrase from a school book.

"That's good," he said, repeating the words after me.

"A land worth fighting for. That's very good indeed." As we walked down the road, he took a shilling from his pocket and handed it to me. The shilling was owing to me in the first place but I didn't think it would come so soon. After the cows were milked, there was another surprise. This time it was for the cows. Instead of turning them into the inches by the small river, I was instructed to allow them into the Fort Field. They truly appreciated the gesture for, when I opened the gate, they thundered past me, bellowing delightedly with their tails cocked high.

In Castleisland, when the football game was over, we repaired to a public house. Country folk, in those days, would leave their custom with traders who hailed originally from their own part of the world, so that when a farmer's son set up a business in a nearby town he could be sure of the support of the folk who came from his own townland and thereabouts.

Men who stand behind the bars of public houses have to be diplomatic or go broke. The publican we visited was no exception. At one time he had been a neighbor of the old man. His greeting was warm and tactful and, when he had dried his hands with a cloth, he extended one to each of us in turn.

"How're the men?" was the first thing he said. This was clever because not only did it embrace us both but it gave

me a dimension for which all boys long. I liked him immediately but, when he winked at me and pulled upon his
waxed mustache, my heart went out to him altogether.

Our drinks were ordered, delivered almost at once, and
paid for.

"Did you start cutting yet?" the publican asked.

"Indeed, I did not," the old man replied, "but, if this
fine spell continues, it could well be that I might be
tempted."

"There's a lot of hay down," a listener put in.

"Meadows are light," the old man countered. "It's
nothing but vanity."

Talk ebbed and flowed. The bar began to fill and as
time went by the speeches grew longer and a little louder.
Men who were silent earlier could not be deterred from
commenting on any and all subjects that came up for discussion.

All round us, postmortems on the game were in full
swing.

"You'll never beat a Tralee team while the ball is dry,"
a man with a pipe in his hand pointed out.

"That may be," said another, "but I tell you that
Castleisland should have made more use of the wings.
When you play the wings you draw the backs and when
you draw the backs you get the openings."

When there was a lull in trade the publican returned to
us. He leaned out over the high counter.

"How many cows are you milking at present?" he
asked.

"Ten," the old man answered.

"Any heifers?"

"Two."

"Calves?"

"Four."

It was plain to see that he had little relish for this sort of conversation. It was altogether too banal and unlikely to strike an interesting note.

"That's a nice field," the publican tried a new tack, "the one with the five-bar gate and the old fort in it."

Immediately, the old man sat bolt upright. The conversation had taken a turn to his liking. The publican, realizing he had scored, pressed home his advantage.

"You could sleep on it," he said, "and you wouldn't know the difference from a mattress."

We were quite taken by this. The old man called for another drink. He included two countrymen who sat on stools beside us.

When farmers meet over a drink, it is not to discuss art or politics, and, when they argue, it is never about religion unless a parish priest is building a new church and is expecting a fixed amount per head of cattle. Farmers talk about the slips and stores and well-bred boars and when they elaborate, which is rarely, they mostly unfold on the theme of drainage grants or certified seed potatoes. Overall, the talk would be of wet land and dry and, when the Fort Field was thrust into the conversation, it was inevitable that it would hold the limelight for a goodly spell.

"There is no field like it in this neck of the woods," the old man announced.

The others nodded sagely and sipped their mediums of porter.

"And I don't mind tellin' you," he went on, "that a lot of folk I could mention has their eye on it."

He submitted the latter part in undertone so that I wouldn't hear for I knew well that there was nobody interested in it but himself.

"I'm told," said the publican, who had returned to us again, "that if you searched it high and low in wintertime you would not find an eggcup of water in it."

"Nor as much as would fill a thimble," the old man supported.

This was followed by a long silence since nobody present could think of anything better to say and so pleasant was the atmosphere and so nicely turned the claims put forward that contradiction would have been sacrilegious. The talk flowed on like a soft stream and subjects from the warble fly to artificial manure were touched upon.

Then, out of the blue, the old man said to nobody in particular, "'Tis a land worth fighting for."

All within earshot cocked their ears at the profundity of this and the two men who had joined us repeated the phrase lovingly lest it be damaged in transit from one mouth to another. Others, out of earshot originally, fastened on it secondhand and uttered it over and over to themselves and to others. The statement puzzled some and a few, not in the know, dismissed it altogether because they could not appreciate the significance of it. By and large it was well received and the majority, although they might never admit it, stored it away for use at some appropriate time in the future.

Before we realized it, the time for closing had come. The publican struck the tall counter three times with a wooden mallet.

"Time for the road, boys," he said.

Without a word, every man downed his drink and quietly we trooped out into the moonlight.

Later on, in bed, the sleep came quickly. It was good to stretch tired limbs on a soft feather tick. I have forgotten what time it was the old woman came into my room. All I recall is waking up to find her hand shaking my shoulder.

"What's up?" I asked drowsily.

"It's that cracked man of mine," she complained. "He can't sleep and wants you out a minute."

I rose and went into the next room. He sat propped by pillows on the bed. His pipe was in his mouth and billows of smoke issued from between his clenched teeth.

"It's gone from me," he said.

"What's gone from you?" I asked.

"What you said this evening about the Fort Field."

"Oh, that," I laughed.

"It's no laughing matter," he said crossly. "I'm awake half the bloody night over it."

"'Tis a land worth fighting for," I reminded him.

He smiled at once and grasped the words as if they were his long lost brothers.

"Ah, yes," he said serenely and he placed his pipe on the bedside table. He flattened the pillows, lay back on the bed and drew the quilt under his chin. A smile of supreme contentment transformed his face.

"A land worth fighting for," he whispered half to himself. Then the snores came and he was deep in sleep.

The Change

The village slept. It was always half asleep. Now, because there was a flaming sun in the June sky, it was really asleep. It consisted of one long street with forty to fifty houses on either side. There were shops, far too many of them, and there were three decaying public houses, the doors of which were closed as if they were ashamed to admit people. No, that isn't quite true. The truth is that passing strangers upset the tenor of normal life. The locals only drank at night, always sparingly, and were therefore reluctant to accept habits that conflicted with their own.

In the center of the roadway a mangy Alsatian bitch sunned herself inconsiderately and that was all the life there was. The day was Friday. I remember it well because my uncle with whom I was staying had cycled to the pier earlier that morning for two fresh mackerel. Mackerel always taste better when they are cooked fresh.

Anyhow, the bitch lay stretched in the sun. From where I sat inside the window of my uncle's kitchen, I could see the street from one end to the other. At nights when he didn't go to the pub, that's what we would do; sit and watch the neighbors from the window. It was his place to comment and I would listen, dodging away to my room sometimes to write down something of exceptional merit. He was a great commentator but I never complimented him. He might stop if I did. It was hard, at times, to keep back the laughter although on rare occasions I was unable to smother it sufficiently and he would look at me suspiciously.

Behind me, I could hear him in the kitchen. He made more noise than was strictly necessary.

"What way do you want it," he called, "boiled or fried?"

"Fried. Naturally."

At the far end of the village a smart green sports car came into view. Its occupants were a boy and a girl. One minute the car was at the end of the street and the next it was braking furiously to avoid collision with the Alsatian bitch.

"What's happening out there?" But he didn't wait for my reply.

He was standing beside me with the frying pan in his hand. The car had stopped and the driver climbed out to remove the obstacle.

"Come on. Come on. Get up out a that, you lazy hound."

Slowly the bitch turned over on her side and scratched the ranges of twin tits which covered her belly. She rose painfully and, without looking at the driver, slunk to the pavement where she immediately lay down again.

By this time a number of people stood in the doorways of their houses. The squeal of brakes had penetrated the entire village and they had come to investigate. I followed my uncle to the doorway where we both stood silently watching the girl. She had eased herself from her seat and was now standing with hands on hips. She was tall and blonde. The tight-fitting red dress she wore clung to her body the way a label sticks to a bottle.

"Very nice. Very nice, indeed," my uncle said.

"I think," the girl told the driver, "I'll take off this dress. I feel clammy."

"Suit yourself," he replied. With that he returned to his seat and lit a cigarette. The red dress was buttoned right down the front.

"What's the name of this place?" she asked as she ripped the topmost button. From the way she said it, we knew that she couldn't care less.

"Don't know," the driver said. Then, as an afterthought, "don't care."

She shrugged her slender shoulders and set to work on the other buttons, oblivious to the wide eyes and partly open mouths of the villagers. A door banged a few houses away but it was the only protest. When she reached the bottom buttons she was forced to stoop but she didn't grunt the way the village women did. Another shrug and the dress flowed from her to the ground.

Underneath she wore checkered shorts and a red bra, no more. The driver didn't even look when she asked him to hand her the sweater which was underneath her seat. Fumbling, his hand located the garment and he tossed it to her. He did make a comment however.

"Godsake hurry up," he said with some irritation.

"Did you ever see such a heartless ruffian?" My uncle folded his arms and there was a dark look on his face. The girl stood for a moment or two shaking dust or motes or some such things from the sweater. Her whole body rippled at every movement. She started to pull the sweater over her head and then an astonishing thing happened. Nobody was prepared for it and this is probably why no one ever spoke about it afterwards. Everybody thought about it afterwards. I'm pretty certain of that.

Quite accidentally, I'm sure of that too, while she was adjusting her neck and shoulders so that she could the better accommodate the sweater, one of her breasts popped out into the sunlight. There were gasps. More doors banged.

A woman's voice called, "Hussy. Hussy."

Obviously she didn't hear. It was a deliciously pink living thing, dun-nippled and vital.

"Do 'em good," my uncle whispered. "Give 'em something to think about."

The sweater in place, the girl adjusted her close-cropped hair. It didn't need adjusting but girls always seem to adjust their hair when it least needs it.

She picked up the dress and with her fingers felt the bonnet of the car. It must have been hot because she took the fingers away quickly and covered the bonnet with the dress. She then sat on the bonnet and from nowhere produced a tube of lipstick. All the while the driver sat looking straight in front of him. He threw the cigarette away before it had burned to the halfway stage. Now he sat with folded arms and hooded eyes that saw nothing.

The girl, her lips glistening, neatly folded the dress, went round to the boot of the car, flicked a button and tucked in the dress. Closing the boot, she looked up and down the street. Her eyes scanned the few remaining faces with interest. If she noticed any reaction, she did not show it in the least. For an instant, her eyes met those of my uncle. He winked almost imperceptibly but she must have noticed it because she permitted herself the faintest glimmer of a smile as she entered the car. She punched the driver playfully and, to give him his due, he caught her round the shoulders and planted a swift kiss on the side of her face. Gears growled throatily and the car leaped forward into sudden life. In an instant it was gone and I was old enough to know that it had gone forever.

Later, when we had eaten our mackerel, we went to drive in the cows for the evening milking. This was the part of the day I liked best. The morning and afternoon hours dragged slowly and lamely but, as soon as the evening milking was done, there was the prospect of some excitement. We could cycle down to the pier and watch the lobster boats arriving home or we could go to the pub and listen.

On that particular evening we decided on the pub. Earlier, while we were eating, he had said that things would never be the same again. "At least," he confided, "not for a hell of a long time anyway." I had pressed him for an explanation.

"Look," he said, "I don't know exactly how to put it but that girl we saw changed things."

"In what way?" I asked.

"Oh, damn," he said, not unkindly, "you have me addled. How do I know in what way? Is this the thanks I get for cooking your mackerel?"

"Aren't you afraid I'll grow up in ignorance?" He was fond of saying this when I failed to show interest in things he considered to be important. But he didn't rise to it. Instead he said: "Wait and see. Wait and see, that's all."

We went to the pub earlier than usual. He shaved before we left the house which was unusual for him. Most men in the village shaved only on Saturday nights or on the eve of holy days.

The pub was cool. There was a long wooden seat just inside the door. We sat and he called for a pint of stout and a bottle of lemonade. There were two other customers. One was a farmer's boy I knew by sight and the other was the young assistant teacher in the local boys' school.

"There was a lot of hay knocked today," the publican said when he had served the drinks and collected his money.

"There was indeed," my uncle answered piously, "and if this weather holds there will be a lot more knocked tomorrow."

I gathered from this that he was at the top of his form. He was saying nothing out of the way. Nobody could possibly benefit from his words. He would go on all night like this relishing the utterly meaningless conversation.

The young teacher who was not a native of the place finished his drink and called for another. There was an unmistakable belligerence about him.

"A chip-carrier," the uncle whispered, "if ever I saw one."

"What about the striptease act today?" the teacher ventured. When no one answered him, he went to the window and looked out.

"Nothing ever happens here," he pouted.

"True for you," said the uncle.

He joined the teacher at the window. The three of us looked out into the street.

"Deserted," the teacher said.

"Terrible," from the uncle.

A couple came sauntering up the street.

"Here's up Flatface," the teacher complained. Flatface

was the name given to Mrs. O'Brien. She had the largest number of children in the village. She wasn't an attractive woman. Neither was her husband an attractive man. But tonight Mrs. O'Brien looked different. She wore make-up and her hair was freshly washed and combed.

"That's a change," my uncle said.

"He'll have her pregnant again," the teacher protested.

Other couples appeared on the street, husbands and wives who were never seen out together. Some were linking arms. All the pairs walked ingratiatingly close to one another.

"What is this?" the teacher asked anxiously, "what's happening?"

"Strange," said the uncle.

Later, when the pub closed, we walked down the street together. On the doorway of the house next to ours, a man and his wife were standing. She wore her Sundays and he leaned heavily on her shoulder.

"I know he's leaning on her," said the uncle, "but for him that's a lot."

Two girls were sitting on the window ledge of the house at the other side.

"Come in for a cup of tea, Jack," one said.

My uncle hesitated.

"Ah, come on, Jack," said the other, "it's early yet."

The young teacher stood at the other side of the street, legs crossed, back propped against the wall. He looked gangly, wretched and lost.

"Care for a drop of tea?" the uncle called across.

Suddenly the teacher sprang into action. He checked first by looking up and down to confirm that it was really he who was being invited. Then, fully assured, he bounded across the roadway, a mad hunger for companionship in his eyes.

The uncle explained to the girls how he would have to see me safely indoors but promised he would be back in a matter of moments. He suggested that meanwhile they start the proceedings without him. Courteously, or rather gallantly, the teacher stood aside to allow the ladies first passage indoors. One giggled but covered her mouth in atonement when the other nudged her to stop. In our own house the uncle poured me a glass of milk and we sat at the table for a spell.

"See what I mean?" he said. "I told you things would never be the same."

I nodded that I fully understood.

"Was that why you shaved tonight?" I asked.

"No," he answered, "but I can see now it was a good job I did."

A Tale of Two Furs

Jack Murphy was a sportsman. By this I mean that it was no trouble at all to him to disappear for a week should there be a succession of sporting events coinciding with a full wallet and a disposition to travel.

He owned a prosperous business and had an excellent wife who always tried to make allowances for him.

He also had a sister-in-law who was forever trying to come between the couple. Jack's was a childless marriage and after fifteen years of "constant endeavor," as he was fond of putting it, there still seemed to be no likelihood of an addition to the family.

The sister-in-law had come to live with them not long after her husband died. Unkind people intimated that she nagged him to death while others held that he drank himself to death to be free of her.

To give him his due, Jack Murphy tolerated her. He never let her feel that she might be an outsider and even his worst enemies were prepared to compliment him on that score. He listened to what she had to say with attentiveness. He would nod politely now and again as she rattled on but he never once indicated by word or gesture whether he agreed with her or not.

Jack's wife Kitty was always expansive in her gratitude to her husband. She was well aware that nobody else would endure Margaretta for so long. She told him so frequently and Jack, because he loved his wife, would always say; "ah 'tis a thing of nothing, Kitty girl. Where else would she go but to her own?"

From the day he quit his teens and inherited the family business, Jack always owned a grayhound or two. Like most grayhound owners he was always patiently waiting for that exceptionally good one to turn up. Sometimes he bred a middling dog or bitch but none had come near equaling any local track records, not to mind breaking one. He persevered. He bought good pups and he mated his brood bitches with the best dogs money could buy. For years he had mixed luck. The most promising pups never lived up to expectations but he was in some way compensated when an average dog ran above himself and won the occasional race.

Then, when he least expected it, he found himself, one season, with a truly talented bitch. She ran unbeaten in her first five starts and qualified, with little difficulty, for the final of an important sweepstake in Ballybunion.

He trained her for the event as he would any other of his charges and she responded by reaching the height of her form at the proper time. At this stage in her career she was well known. Sportswriters in the national dailies and evening papers predicted a bright future. Like the true doggy man he was, Jack Murphy kept his mind to himself. He had high hopes but it would never do to divulge these. The prospect of a big let-down in the long term was always on the cards. As the day of the sweepstake final drew near, he was tempted to consult local handlers but, on the advice of his veterinary, he decided to trust to the bitch's natural talents.

On the morning of the big event, Jack took his car to the garage and had it greased and cleaned. As he drove back to his home, friends and neighbors stood in their doorways and wished him good luck for the night. He acknowledged each and every salute. Somehow he felt that a new responsibility had been thrust upon him. He was possessed of the natural fatalism of all grayhound fanciers but now, for the first time, he realized that his fellow townsfolk had entrusted him with the onerous task of improving the town's image. Many would be making the journey later that evening to cheer the bitch to victory but

Jack was the captain so to speak. He was the very spearhead of the assault.

At home in the kitchen, he kissed his wife goodbye. She held him longer than was normal for her. She knew that this was one of the most important occasions in his life. Finally she released him and from the folds of her purse withdrew a small bottle. It was partly filled with blessed water which a thoughtful neighbor had brought back from Lourdes. She allowed a few drops to spill over her fingertips. This she applied to his forehead, making the sign of the cross as she did so. She sprinkled the remainder of the water on the bitch. At this stage, Margaretta entered the kitchen. Jack knew she would be incapable of wishing him good luck. It was not in her make-up.

"I'll be back some time tonight," he told his wife, "or, if not, I'll be here early tomorrow."

"We all know the words of that song," the sister-in-law announced to nobody in particular.

"Now, now," said Kitty, "that will do you. 'Twould be more in your line to wish him luck."

"Luck is the grace of God," Margaretta retorted sharply. Jack refused to be drawn into the argument.

"You can get Timmy Kelliher to walk the other dogs," he told his wife. "Tell him I'll fix up with him tomorrow night."

Saying not another word, he led the dog from the kitchen. He had already removed the cushions from the back seat of the car and covered the floor with a good depth of fresh straw.

"You and me," he confided to the wide-awake hound, "will show the lot of 'em a thing or two tonight." Then he drove off, not heeding now the God-speeds and the waving hands. He was gone but seconds from the kitchen when the sisters had it hot and heavy between them.

"God knows when we'll see him again," Margaretta spouted, "it could be days and it could be weeks and then again he might take it into his napper to come back no more. I wouldn't put it past him now that he has the broad road between him and his home."

"He said he'd be back tonight," Kitty replied testily, "and back he'll be."

"So you say," said Margaretta, "but I expect the likes of that when I see it before me."

"It's none of your business anyway," Kitty cut her short. "He's the boss of this house and I don't know where you get the right to criticize him."

"Oh, you needn't tell me who's the boss here," Margaretta shouted back. "I know my place. I've been put there often enough."

The argument wore itself out after a while but nothing was settled. There was always the danger that it would flare up again.

Ballybunion track was crowded for the feature event of the night, the sweepstake final. The bitch was quoted liberally enough but her price shortened as Jack's friends and neighbors began to arrive. Eventually she was installed a firm favorite at five to four. Jack had been fortunate to get her at fours as soon as the prices went on the boards. He had on twenty-five pounds which meant that he stood to win a hundred pounds in addition to the two hundred and fifty pounds stake money should the bitch cross the line first.

As before all big events, there was a sudden silence when the field of six were placed in their respective boxes. The tension mounted as the hare whistled up to the traps and when the dogs broke there was a mighty cheer, each of six contingents shouting for its fancy. The bitch broke well and was second as they came round the first bend.

At the second bend, she was third and, at the third, she was in exactly the same place. Now the roars of the crowd were intensified and women could be heard screaming as the dogs entered the straight. It was here the bitch showed her real talent. She saw an opening next to the rails, took it like a flash and with it the lead for the first time. She won comfortably.

From all sides Jack was pummeled and patted by well-wishers. Supporters fought with each other to shake his hand. Jack said little. The one phrase he kept repeating to nobody in particular was "What did I tell you? What did I tell you?"

He kept saying this over and over until his admirers departed to draw their money from the bookies.

An hour after the race, Jack was entrenched in the corner of a public house lounge with a large number of friends seated protectively around him. At his feet sat the bitch. Under his seat was the trophy, a solid silver cup with the figures of six grayhounds inscribed around its middle. In his wallet was the money he had collected from the book-maker. Also there was the check for two hundred and fifty pounds from the sweepstake. The cup had been filled and refilled with brandy and champagne.

Jack Murphy felt good. He had never felt so good before. In his hand was a glass of whiskey. He dipped his fingers in the glass and rubbed them against the bitch's mouth. Her reaction was to lift her head and look around wide-eyed at the strange faces. All were loud in praise of her performance.

"What did I tell you?" Jack Murphy said. "What did I tell you?"

A tall figure entered the lounge and a hush fell. People nodded respectfully and drifted aside as he moved towards Jack and the sitting hound.

This was Mister McKechnick, the English buyer. He was as well known on Irish dog tracks as he was on Eng-lish ones. He was known to be a decent man and conse-quently he was admired and respected wherever he went. He had a good name as a buyer. It was said of him that he never looked for bargains. He always paid what a dog was worth, no more and no less.

He beckoned to the barman.

"Fill a drink for the house," he said quietly. When his bidding was done, all present drank his health. Then Jack Murphy rose from his seat. He was a trifle unsteady but he was far from being drunk.

"Fill them up again," he said to the barman.

"You have a class bitch there, sir," McKechnick complimented him.

"Thank you, sir," Jack returned. The two men chatted amiably while those within earshot respectfully withdrew. Business was business and nobody wished to stand in the way of a fair deal.

"What would you say she's worth?" McKechnick asked out of the blue.

"You're too sudden for me," Jack answered. "I would have to think that one over for a while."

"Put some sort of estimate on her," McKechnick urged.

Jack pursed his lips and scratched his head. He looked at the bitch and he looked at McKechnick. He looked at the floor and he looked at the ceiling. He looked at the serious, expectant faces ranged around the lounge and yet he was reluctant to fix a price. He realized that McKechnick was not a dawdler. Rather was he a busy man with little time on his hands.

"I would say, sir," said Jack in his most earnest fashion, "that she's worth every penny of twelve hundred quid."

"What would you say to nine hundred?" the Englishman asked with a smile.

"I would say eleven hundred," Jack responded with another smile.

"It looks rather like a thousand then, don't it?" McKechnick said with a hearty laugh.

"It do indeed," Jack answered with another laugh.

McKechnick extended his hand and Jack took it in his. There was a handclap from the crowd.

"I'll give you my check," McKechnick whispered,

"when things quieten down a little."

Jack nodded agreement. McKechnick beckoned to a small, mustached man at the door.

"My man will take charge of her now," he said.

As the bitch was being led away, Jack suddenly bent down and impulsively flung his arms round her.

"Goodbye, my little darling," he said with tears in his eyes. "Goodbye and good luck to you."

At McKechnick's suggestion, Jack accompanied him to his hotel. In the residents' lounge, the Englishman handed over the check. Jack took a ten pound note from his wallet and thrust it into McKechnick's pocket by way of a luck penny. After that, they had several drinks.

"You'll be my guest for the night of course," McKechnick suggested. Jack had no objection. At twelve the Englishman announced that he was about to retire.

"I'm going to Limerick Races tomorrow," he explained, "and I don't want a hangover for the day."

"I'm bound for those very same races," Jack revealed, "so I think I'll hit the sack too."

In Limerick they fared well. During the two days of the races, they backed several winners. McKechnick had good connections and the information he received proved most valuable. At night they would do the round of the city's pubs, joining in sing-songs and making new friends. On the final night there were several in the party. They had a hectic time between dancing and singing. Bottle after bottle of champagne was drunk. At midnight, McKechnick announced that he proposed to withdraw on the grounds that he intended traveling to the Curragh Races on the morrow. He asked Jack if he would care to accompany him. On the spur of the moment, Jack agreed.

Quite a large party left Limerick for the Curragh the following morning. Jack rode with McKechnick, a titled lady who owned several racehorses, a bookmaker and two unattached, middle-aged ladies, friends of the titled lady.

Their good luck held at the Curragh. They had a golden rule about daytime drinking. Under no circumstances was anybody to touch a drop until five-thirty in the afternoon. McKechnick had a theory that betting and drinking did not go hand in hand. They had bets on four races. They won on three.

McKechnick declared more than once that Jack had brought them good luck. At five-thirty they repaired to the Grandstand bar where they proceeded to drink gins and tonics. After an hour, the party was a merry one.

At six-thirty, the titled lady got on the phone to a Dublin theater and booked seats for the night's performance of a play which, she told Jack, had been favorably reviewed in all the dailies of the previous Tuesday. Jack slept soundly throughout the performance. He was loud in his praise after the final curtain had come down.

He remembered little after that. The night passed in a haze. During a meal in one of the city's more celebrated hotels he fell fast asleep. When he woke up he found himself in strange surroundings. He was in a comfortable bed in a bright, fully carpeted room. There was a chambermaid, dressed all in white, shaking his shoulder.

"They said I was to call you not later than half-past eleven, sir," the chambermaid informed him.

"Who said?" Jack asked.

"Your friends, sir. It's Sunday and last Mass is at twelve. I've brought you some tea. I'll leave it here."

She carefully placed the tray of tea things on a chair near the bed. Then she left the room quietly. Painfully, Jack raised his head from the pillows. More painfully still, he eased himself from the bed. He dressed slowly as though his body was covered with sores and needed to be treated with the utmost gentleness. He found his way downstairs and thence to the church.

Mass went by like a dream. It gave him all he could do to rouse himself at its conclusion. He struggled back to the hotel, went directly upstairs and straight to bed. The next time he woke, he felt refreshed. He located his clothes and went through the pockets. His money was intact. He lay back on the bed, glad that it had not been stolen.

Then, for the first time in days, he remembered his wife and, as soon as he thought of her, he thought of Margaretta. He could sense her gloating in the background. Thinking about his wife filled him with remorse. He could see the hurt in her eyes as the sister lorded it over her. There came a knock upon the bedroom door, gentle yet firm.

"Come in," Jack called. It was the chambermaid who had awakened him the morning before. Again she carried a tray.

"What day have we?" Jack asked.

"It's Monday, sir."

"Great God almighty!" Jack exclaimed, "and will you tell me what time is it?"

"It's eight o'clock in the morning, sir."

Upon hearing this, he groaned and buried his face in his hands. He ran his fingers through his hair and groaned again and again.

"Is something up, sir?" the chambermaid's voice was filled with alarm.

"I wish I was dead," said Jack Murphy.

For the first time he noticed the girl. She was young, no more than eighteen, but she had a sympathetic face and sympathy was exactly what Jack needed just then. The source did not worry him. While she poured his tea, he launched into a full account of his adventures. She listened carefully and when he had finished she nodded her head sagely.

"I wouldn't worry too much," she told him. "You still have the money and that's a good start."

"Oh, sure," he said with an edge of sarcasm, "but 'tis me and not you that has to face the music."

"All you have to do," she told him bluntly, "is buy a fur coat for your wife. I promise you there won't be a word out of her if you land back with a good quality fur coat."

"A fur coat," he said and pondered her suggestion.

"But where would I get one?"

"Look," she said kindly, "I have an hour off at twelve. If you like, I could meet you outside and show you where to go."

"Good God," said Jack gratefully, "that would be great, great entirely."

At twelve o'clock, she was as good as her word. At ten past, they were walking up Grafton Street. At half past, they had narrowed the selection down to two.

One was a musquash at one hundred and fifty pounds and the other a Canadian squirrel at one hundred and forty. They decided upon the musquash.

"Listen," said the salesman confidently. He spoke as if he were doing them a very considerable personal favor.

"Why not take both? You pay for them now. When you arrive home, let her decide for herself. You can return the one she doesn't want and we will only be happy to refund your money."

This seemed to be an excellent idea.

"There is one other thing," said Jack Murphy to the salesman, "my wife is a very thrifty sort of woman so, like a good man, will you knock down the prices a bit."

"We shall have no problem at all in that respect," the salesman assured them. He produced two price tags, one marked thirty and the other twenty-five pounds. He attached the thirty pound tag to the musquash and the twenty-five to the Canadian squirrel. Jack returned with his parcels to the hotel where he bade goodbye to his young friend. He thrust a ten pound note into her hand as they parted.

It was late that night when he arrived home. It goes without saying that he was coolly received. His wife had no word of welcome for him, no word that is, until he produced the parcels. Proudly he ripped them open. He presented her with the musquash, explaining that the other was on appro.

His wife was enchanted. She pressed the coat against her body and caressed it with her free hand.

That night, Jack Murphy slept the sleep of the just. In the morning, he received his breakfast in bed. His wife sat on the edge, fondly watching him as he ate.

"I have good news for you," she said.

"What would that be?" Jacked asked absently.

"You needn't bother to return the other coat. Margaretta thinks it a steal at twenty-five pounds and she's decided to keep it."

The Hanging

There is no sight so grotesque or pathetic as the dangling frame of a hanged man. It is also an affront to human symmetry. There is no parody so wretched and, when Billy Fitz and John Murphy first saw Denny Bruder's body hanging from the crossbeam in Looney's shed, they were bemused for some moments by the almost comic presentation of slack hands and slanted head. From the church nearby, as if by arrangement, came the muted tolling of the Angelus bell.

Billy moved first. He touched the hanging foot nearest him and, when nothing happened, he pushed it gingerly with his palm. The body unexpectedly started to gyrate slowly. The screams of the boys were simultaneous. They ran terrified from the shed.

Denny Bruder had first come to the village about five years before. He was a motor mechanic by trade. He took a lease of Looney's shed and, in a short while, built a reputation as an efficient man who knew all there was to be known about motor cars. You could not call him morose. Glum would be a more fitting word. He was gentle with children and he never resented their curiosity. He was not the best of mixers and mostly he was to be seen alone going for walks or visiting the cinema where pictures were shown every other night.

In the beginning, he was never known to enter a public house and he showed little interest in the local girls but this could have been because they showed little interest in him. He was not the handsomest of men. He was medium-sized with a rather bulbous nose and thick lips. However, he was far from being repulsive. His was a dour sort of face. Older women in the village described it as homely. In time, people came to accept him as part of the local scene.

Shortly after Denny Bruder's arrival, Imogen Furey invested in a second-hand car. Imogen was the wife of Jack Furey, the cattle-jobber. Jack already had a car but, as Imogen told anybody who might be prepared to listen, he was away from home so often at cattle fairs all over the country that they might as well not have a car at all. While Jack was away, Imogen would visit his fields outside the village to count the cattle and to see if any wandering animals had broken down fences or forced entry. She would do this in all kinds of weather and, since the fields were the best part of a mile from the village, she was often in receipt of a discomfiting drenching and this, in addition to the time wasted, was one of the chief reasons why she felt the need of the car. There were two children, both girls, but these were away at boarding school for most of the year.

The car was an old model and, if it burned more than its quota of oil, it suited Imogen's needs nicely. When it broke down one evening as she was returning from counting the cattle, she sent for Denny Bruder who towed it to his shed. It transpired that the fan belt was broken. There was nothing else the matter. While Denny was installing a new belt, Imogen suggested that he give the car a complete overhaul. She left it in his care and, late the following afternoon, he delivered it to her door. She was surprised at the reasonableness of his fee.

Thereafter, they became good friends and he took a personal interest in the behavior of the car.

Midway through his second year, Denny Bruder invested in some up-to-date garage equipment. This improved his business considerably and, in his third year, he found himself with more money than he actually needed. He looked about for a safe spot to invest it.

It was Imogen Furey who solved his problem. Envious neighbors were fond of saying that she knew everything about everybody. By this they inferred that she knew more than was good for her. Uncharitably they would hint that if she paid more time to her own business and less to the business of others she would be better off. This, of course, was not the case at all. Imogen Furey was an eminently successful woman by any standards. Her husband was reputed to be the wealthiest man in the village. Her home had every conceivable amenity. She dressed well and was a leading figure on local committees. Her children were boarded at one of the most exclusive schools in the country. On the surface, at any rate, hers was the sort of thoroughly satisfying existence which was bound to provoke resentment and jealousy.

When Denny Bruder confided to her that he had money to spare, she asked for time to consider his situation. It was her experience that house property or land were the safest means of ensuring a profitable return from investment. On the outskirts of the village was a two-storied house in relatively good condition. It had been on the market for some years but, because its owner was asking too exorbitant a price, it went unsold. She informed Denny that she was convinced the house could be bought for the sum originally asked. After an interval of three years, she explained that the price was not in the least exorbitant by prevailing values.

Denny bought the house, handed notice to his landlady and moved in. For months, he was rarely seen in public. After work, he would spend most of his time indoors, redecorating the rooms and generally restoring the woodwork, ceilings and anything else he found in disrepair. When he had finished indoors, he started on the outside. It was early spring when he started on the neglected garden which faced the roadway. He planted shrubs and trees and showed an excellent sense of taste in his selections.

He painted the house front and windows with delicately contrasting shades. By late spring, the job was completed. He was more than satisfied with his handiwork. He decided to sit back and await developments. All through the summer, he confidently expected a proposal or suggestion of marriage through some medium from whatever candidates were available. The house was his chief bait. It was much admired by the villagers, as was the garden. He worked hard and, which was more important, he was seen to work hard. He bought new clothes and invested in a small comfortable car. The months of summer wore on and when the trees began to shed the first autumn leaves he found himself still with an empty house. He was puzzled. He knew he was no ladykiller but he was also aware that there were many happily married men in the village far uglier and less well-off.

He started to visit the public houses. He never drank more than a glass or two of beer. He became friendly with some of the barmaids but that was as far as it went. He went to dances in the village hall and sometimes to neighboring towns when the bigger, better-known bands included these in their itineraries. He never danced. He often tried but the girls he fancied were snapped up before he could get off his mark. Consequently, he spent most of his time standing with other male onlookers at the rear of the hall.

That winter was one of the most miserable he ever spent. He missed the company of the other lodgers in his old digs. The house was unbearably lonely. To crown his misfortune, he was smitten by a heavy dose of influenza. He was three days in his bed before anybody showed sufficient interest in his whereabouts to pay a visit to the house. His friend Imogen Furey eventually called. He thrust a muffled head from one of the uppermost windows and told her hoarsely that he was ill. At her bidding, he dropped the key to the door at her feet. She was back in less than half an hour with a jug of chicken broth. She called again and again until he was fit to resume work.

At Christmas, to repay her kindness, he bought her a present of the most expensive perfume available. The Fureys, to give them their due, knew a decent man when they met one. At Jack's bidding, Imogen invited Denny to a meal one of the nights during Christmas. Afterwards, they sat in front of the sittingroom fire drinking a special punch compounded by Imogen. The heat of the fire and the whiskey to which he was unused had the effect of totally loosening Denny's tongue. In a short while, he had unfolded his tale of woe, confessing his loneliness and explaining his most pressing need.

The Fureys were moved first to concern and then to pity. At a late hour that night, Jack Furey drove Denny home. In bed later on, he asked his wife if there was anything she could do.

"He's a likely fellow," Jack said, "and by the cut of him I don't think he'd blackguard a girl."

"He's no Romeo," Imogen pointed out.

"Romeo's don't always make the best husbands," Jack countered. Before she slept, she promised she would look into it.

THE HANGING

"I'll have to think of who's available," she said thoughtfully. Jack Furey knew his wife.

"You'll come up with something," he announced sleepily.

Through the spring, Denny planted more shrubs and blooms. At his garage, he worked hard. He had, by now, acquired more than a local reputation and motorists from neighboring towns would patronize him occasionally. He took to dealing in second-hand cars and was soon making more than he ever dreamed possible. He bought a better car and went about more. On Saint Patrick's night, he was invited to a party at Fureys. There were other people present. One of these was a girl from the nearby hill country. Her name was Nora Odell. She was auburn-haired and, although exceedingly pale of feature, was nevertheless quite an attractive girl in her late twenties. She was an indrawn, reserved sort. There had been talk that she had been seriously let down once by a neighboring farmer but this was discounted as immaterial since almost everybody is subject to some sort of letdown at one time or another, the only difference being that there is never much revelation of these reverses by those who are at the receiving end.

Towards midnight, all present gathered round the piano in the Furey sittingroom. Denny Bruder surprised everybody by proving himself to be the proprietor of a very fine baritone voice. The evening was a success. At Imogen Furey's suggestion, Denny asked Nora Odell if he might call and take her out some time. She agreed and they settled upon a date. Unfortunately, it was a blustery, rainy night.

For want of something better to do, Denny asked her if she would like to see the interior of his house. At first, she was reluctant but he seemed so genuinely put out that she relented.

After a tour of the bedrooms, he asked her if she would like to hear some records. He injected life into the sitting-groom fire and chose a selection of Strauss waltzes. The evening was a happy one. She often came to the house after that.

Once he invited her to dinner. He prepared it himself. The main course consisted of curried chicken with the faintest echo of garlic for which she did not exactly care. Otherwise it was a first class meal. Denny explained that, during his school holidays, he used to help his mother in the kitchen of the hotel where she worked during the summer. He was an excellent cook and she would seize eagerly upon his invitations to dine in the house. Knowing her dislike of garlic, he never used it when she was joining him for a meal. As the months went by, Denny Bruder began to fall inextricably in love with Nora Odell. He never told her so. He was content to bide his time and wait for a suitable opportunity. Summer came and, on Sundays, they would motor to the seaside. Sometimes he would take her father and mother. He was now a constant caller at the Odell home. The senior Odells liked him and Nora's brothers respected him. He was one of the best mechanics for miles and a chap never knew when he might be obliged to visit him.

One fine Sunday in August, the pair sat on the grass at the end of a peaceful headland overlooking the sea. Beneath them, the incoming tide was noiseless and the flat unbroken surface of the sea like a sheet of silver. Overhead the sun shone from a blue sky. Suddenly Denny Bruder placed an arm around Nora Odell's shoulder.

"I'd love if you married me," he said.

"Would you?" she asked, turning and looking at him directly.

"You know very well I would," he told her.

"Kiss me," Nora said. He kissed her awkwardly. After the kiss, she took his hand and led him to the shore where the small waves broke listlessly at their feet.

"I'll have to tell my parents," she said, "and you will have to speak to my father, ask for my hand, if you know what I mean."

"That will be no bother," Denny assured her.

"I'm sure he'll be pleased," she said, as if she had known all along that their marriage was inevitable.

Denny Bruder was elated. Without taking off his shoes he ran in the water up to his knees and shouted to the heavens. "I'm going to be married," he called out. "I'm going to be married to Nora Odell."

They became engaged a fortnight later and a date was set for the wedding. Neither approved of long engagements and so it was that they decided upon the first Saturday of October. In early September, however, they were to be separated for a longish period. Nora's sister Bridie, who was married in Wolverhampton, was due to have her third child about this time. She wrote to Nora asking her to come and housekeep for her husband and two children.

Denny drove her to Rosslare which was the port most

convenient. As he kissed her goodbye, he suddenly realized how utterly empty his future would be without her. She had given his life a new meaning. He was, in fact, a different person since meeting her. People had told him so. It was expected she would be gone for a fortnight. This would allow her a week to prepare for the wedding upon her return home.

During her absence, Denny spent every second night visiting the cinema. He always occupied the same seat in the balcony. One night a woman called Angela Fell, the wife of a local shopkeeper, happened to be seated next to him. Midway through the film, she suddenly said, "Oh, oh" She said it loudly so that her voice carried to the corners of the balcony. Then she left her seat and occupied another at the end of the last row. After the show, there was much conjecture. Several different reasons were put forward to justify the uncharacteristic behavior of Angela Fell. Those who sat nearest to Denny Bruder spoke from a position of authority. A young man who sat directly behind Mrs. Fell said that Denny was seen to lift his hand suddenly when she uttered the exclamation already described. As to the exact location of the hand prior to its being lifted, he was heard to say, "where the hell do you think it was?"

By implication this meant that Denny Bruder's hand was placed on an area of Angela Fell's anatomy which might best be described as out of bounds. There were some who flatly refused to believe this. There were others who refused to believe otherwise. Nobody thought of asking Angela Fell. Of all the women in the village she was the least communicative and the sharpest-tongued.

After this incident Denny Bruder was a marked man. People in his vicinity on the balcony would be paying more attention to him than to the screen. Denny had no idea he was under observation. A week passed and a teenage girl from the nearby countryside arrived late at the cinema. She fumbled her way to a vacant seat next to Denny Bruder. Couples nudged each other in anticipation. Nothing happened till near the end of the film. Then she left her seat and went outside. There was no longer any doubt in the minds of the villagers.

Some were filled with pity, others with indignation. Imogen Furey found herself in a dilemma. It was she who introduced Nora Odell to Denny. Clearly, she would have to do something. One night in bed, she asked Jack if he was asleep. He had been away for several days buying calves in the western counties and had earlier retired to bed. Jack Furey was awake. Painfully, Imogen related the details of what had transpired in the cinema.

"What am I to do?" she asked.

"Leave well alone," Jack Furey advised her, "marriage will knock all that sort of thing out of him."

"I feel responsible," Imogen persisted.

Jack lay silent. He could feel sympathy for Denny Bruder. He remembered what it was to be lonely, to be so sick with desire that little was beyond contemplation. Essentially he was a tolerant man who was prepared to go out of his way to make allowances.

"I once caught a girl by the knee in the cinema," he said trying to make light of the matter.

"But you knew her," Imogen replied.

"I thought I knew her," Jack Furey said, "she was no damned good."

Imogen knuckled him playfully on the side of the face. "It's no laughing matter," she said seriously, "I wish to God it was."

They spoke far into the night. At Jack's suggestion, she agreed to do or say nothing until Nora came home. Shortly before her return, Nora received two anonymous letters. The day before her actual departure, she received a telegram from her older brother which stated coldly that he would be meeting her at Rosslare. She had been prepared to discount the two letters until she read the telegram.

It had been agreed that Denny Bruder would meet her. If her family saw fit to change the arrangement, there must be something afoot. Both brothers were waiting when she disembarked. There and then they made her pen a letter to Denny acquainting him of a change of mind on her part. At first, she refused point blank but when they threatened to deal with Denny themselves she reluctantly agreed. She would have liked to hear his side of the story. Family was family however and in the end where else was a person to fall back. She succeeded in convincing herself that she was doing the correct thing. In the days that followed, Denny Bruder called repeatedly at the Odell farmhouse. He refused to stop calling even when the older brother appeared at the front door one evening with a shotgun in his hands. In the end, both brothers dealt him a severe beating.

After this, he concealed himself for a time. It was when word of the beating reached the Furey household that Imogen decided to act. Jack had left early that morning. Before his departure, he asked Imogen to pay a visit to Nora Odell.

"If either of them two brothers so much as looks at you sideways, I won't like it and you can tell 'em so."

Imogen nodded. As soon as Jack had gone she made out a shopping list. Shortly before noon she betook herself to Fell's grocery. Mick Fell carefully scrutinized her order which was a substantial one.

"I'd like a word with Angela while you're getting those ready," Imogen said.

"Of course," Mick Fell agreed. "Go straight through."

Imogen followed a narrow passageway into a tiny kitchen. It was a suffocating place with a gleaming hot Stanley range dominating the entire scene from one corner. Angela was bent over a small table chopping meat.

"I hope I haven't come at a bad time," Imogen said.

Without a word, Angela strode past her towards the shop. Imogen could hear her voice plainly. "I thought I told you I didn't want to see anybody while I was working. What sort of goddamned nit are you anyway?"

"Look at the size of the order she's given me," Mick Fell replied defensively.

"I don't care if she gave you herself," Angela screamed at him. "I don't want people collaring me in that hellhole."

"What do you want of me?" she asked with hands on hips when she returned.

"Simply this," Imogen answered tonelessly, "what did Denny Bruder do to you at the cinema?"

"You have a blasted neck, you have," Angela hit out.

"His hopes of marriage are wrecked," Imogen forestalled her. "Tell me what really happened. I promise you no one else will ever know."

"Get out of here," Angela advanced a step. Imogen refused to give ground.

"I'm not leaving this kitchen till you tell me," she declared. "A man's whole future depends on what you say to me this morning. I'm asking you, as one mother to another, if Denny Bruder molested you in any way that night at the pictures. If he is innocent, you have a duty to perform. If not, say so and I'll walk out of here this instant."

"I have nothing to say to you," Angela returned. "Please leave now."

Imogen took a step in the direction of the shop but turned finally and faced Angela squarely.

"If this gets into court," she said, "and it well may, you won't get off so lightly."

The veneer of hard independence faded from Angela's face. "Court," she echoed stupidly.

"Yes, court," Imogen pressed her advantage. "That's where they take people who destroy a person's character."

"I've destroyed nobody's character. I never put a hard word on the man."

"That may be but you never put a good word on him either."

They stood facing each other. From the shop came the voices of other customers. There was laughter when Mick Fell passed a wry remark. Angela crossed to the table where she resumed her chopping. She spoke over her shoulder. "He did nothing to me," she said. "I left my seat because there was a smell of garlic. When he belched, I found it overpowering so I went to another seat."

"You might have said so before this," Imogen said accusingly. In the shop, she collected her groceries. She resolved to go to Odells that afternoon. First she would see Denny Bruder. Not for the first time she marveled at the unnatural reticence of women like Angela Fell. Involuntarily she shuddered when she thought of the evil begat by the silence of such people.

As she crossed the roadway to her home, the Angelus rang. She blessed herself as did others who were on the streets. Between the peals, she could hear the distant cries of children.

Jonathan

The rhododendrons were in full bloom. White and scarlet and puce, profuse and gay, they brightened the long avenue that led to the old house. He could not see it yet but any moment now it would present itself. Surely it would be round the next bend. It seemed as if he had been walking for miles and miles, for hours and hours. It wasn't the tiredness that bothered him. It was the boredom. He had not met a single creature since entering the avenue a half hour before. He had spent most of the time dawdling, feeling the texture of the rhododendron petals or descending the grassy slope to plop pebbles into the stream which accompanied the avenue from the beginning.

Jonathan was eleven. He was small for his age but well-knit with good bones. From time to time, he would change the letter from one hand to the other. That was the whole purpose of his journey, the letter. He knew its contents by heart, not because he had opened it but because he was partly responsible for its composition.

He had helped Paddy Pine to write it. Paddy worked with Jonathan's father on the farm and lived in the farmhouse where he had a room of his own overlooking the river. He was an orphanage boy although he was now more of a man having passed the twenty mark some months previously. He was fifteen when he first came to work with the Hindleys. Paddy Pine was a runaway. With another boy he scaled the orphanage wall one night and ran off to join the British army. That was in nineteen forty-one. An astonished Russia had just been invaded by a rampant Germany and the British recruiting offices were none too inquisitorial when a likely prospect proffered himself for enlistment. It was Paddy's intention to walk the two hundred miles from Kerry to the border town of Castleblayney. From there to the recruiting office in Newry on the other side of the border would be a mere formality. On their second day out, they ran short of food and, without letting him know, Paddy's friend returned to the orphanage. This did not deter him. He resolved to go on. On the morning of the third day, Hilary Hindley, Jonathan's mother, found him in one of the outhouses. He was in high fever. It was almost a week before he was able to stand by himself. The kindness shown him by the Hindleys was something he could not fully comprehend. They had never seen him before. They owed him nothing yet while he was ill they tended to his every want. The children, young Jonathan and the twins Rose and Sheila who were a year older, spent all of their free time reading to him during his convalescence. As the days went happily by, he began to feel guilty and fearful. There would be a hot reception awaiting him at the orphanage. He resolved to make a second break for the border at the first opportunity. He felt an unbearable pang of loneliness at the prospect of leaving the Hindleys. It was a thought he dared not dwell upon.

On the night before his planned departure, Ned Hindley took him aside.

"I should have reported finding you to the civic guards, Paddy," Ned started, "but I couldn't find it in my heart to do it just then. I've kept putting it off and off but now the time has come when I have to."

Paddy Pine said nothing. He nodded his head in resignation while Ned Hindley continued.

"If you still want to hit for the border, the door is open to you and I'll see to it you get a good start with enough food and a pound or two in your pocket."

"I want to stay here. I'll be your workman. I'll do anything," Paddy cried out the words in anguish. Hilary Hindley came running from the kitchen.

"What did you do to him?" she said accusingly. She

hurried towards Paddy and placed her arms round him protectively.

"I did nothing," Ned Hindley said with a pained face. "I just told him the score and he said he wanted to stay here. That's all."

"If that's what he wants, then that's the way it's going to be," Hilary announced firmly.

"That might not be possible," her husband warned.

"Well," she said, "you'd better make it possible or you'll be sleeping alone for a while."

Ned Hindley knew his wife well enough to know that she meant what she said. Only once before did she issue such an ultimatum and, when he failed to take her seriously, he was left out in the cold for an unbearably long time.

"I'll do what I can," he promised. There had been difficulties but the Hindleys were held in high regard locally and, after a short, concessive period in the orphanage, Paddy Pine was duly released into their hands. He had two qualities which endeared him to Ned and Hilary from the beginning. The boy was refreshingly innocent and absolutely loyal. On the debit side he was not the brightest boy in the world and, before he could grasp even the most elementary chore, the directions had to be hammered home repeatedly. This apart, he was an able and willing farmhand and was completely happy at his work. As he grew older, his shyness became more pronounced. He found it difficult to communicate with girls and despite every help from Ned and Hilary he made little headway in this field.

"Don't worry," Ned said to his wife, "when the right one comes along there'll be no holding him."

"Yes," she said seriously, "but will he recognize the right one when he sees her?"

Time passed and Jenny Stevens entered Paddy Pine's life. It was to be some time before Jenny was to know about it. Paddy noticed her first at Mass. On a number of occasions, she smiled at him but she would have no way of knowing his true feelings. She was the youngest of a large local family and, as soon as she reached school-leaving age, she was pressed into domestic service with a neighboring farmer. The work was hard and the hours long. After a year, she tired of it and found employment with the Misses Carter, Julie and Emily, who lived in the old house in what was left of the Carter demesne. Here, the work was much lighter and hours shorter. Here too, she was not discouraged when she used make-up or affected what the local people interpreted as airs and graces.

It was to the Carter house Jonathan was presently bound with the letter from Paddy Pine to Jenny Stevens. The contents of the letter were simple enough, an appeal without embellishments asking her to attend the Sunday night dance in the Parochial hall.

It was a task to Jonathan's liking. He reveled in any sort of intrigue and this, in his estimation, was intrigue of a high order. Suddenly, the old house thrust itself into view. Three-stories, ivy-covered and Georgian, it stood elegantly and correctly at the end of the avenue. Built in 1820 by the great-grandfather of the present owners, its regency facade at once impressed the visitor. Giant, ancient oaks and chestnuts stood aloofly and discreetly at either side, dwarfing the rhododendrons which spread out to left and right around a graveled frontage. In terms of character and distinction, it easily outdid all the other residences in the parish.

The demesne consisted of two hundred acres. One hundred and fifty of these were of the finest pasture-land. The other fifty were mostly woodland and scrub. It was the biggest holding for miles. In various local histories, it was rather unflatteringly referred to as a typical Ascendancy dwelling-house. Whatever one may think of this, the land was certainly Ascendancy-type in that it was the most fertile in the district.

"Fair play to the English," Jonathan had once heard his father say, "they never stole anything but the best."

There was no ill-feeling in the way he said it. It was purely good-natured resignation. Jonathan stood for a while where the avenue expanded and ended in the gravel frontage. He imagined all sorts of things. Who dared guess what baleful eyes might be peering at him from one of the large windows or what fiendish goings-on were carefully concealed behind the huge oaken door? In the nearby rhododendrons, there was a faint stirring followed by an awesome silence. He bent noiselessly and selected a polished rounded stone. Taking careful aim, he lobbed it into the exact spot in the bushes where the sound had come from. Suddenly, explosively, a pair of protesting blackbirds erupted from the depths, chattering insanely till they found sanctuary further down the avenue. The noise attracted a figure from the rear of the house. It was Miss Emily, the younger of the Carter sisters. Emily Carter was in her early seventies. In one hand, she carried a book and, in the other, an ancient walking stick which she threateningly held aloft.

When she saw who it was, she lowered the stick. "I thought it might be a stray dog," she explained, "they come all the time to chase the cattle."

"Who is it, Emily?" her sister's voice called from the side of the house.

"It's only Hilary Hindley's Jonathan," Emily called back.

"What does he want?" Miss Julie asked as soon as she saw Jonathan.

"What is it you want?" Emily asked.

"I have a message for Jenny Stevens," Jonathan replied. Upon hearing this, both women exchanged knowing glances.

"I hope we have not come on a mission of maid-filching," Miss Julie said crossly. It was some time before Jonathan was able to comprehend this.

"My mother never has a maid," he answered, after a while, in what he hoped was an equally cross tone.

"There's always a first time," Miss Julie shot back.

"I have a letter from Paddy Pine for Miss Stevens," Jonathan blurted out, "as soon as I give it to her, I'll be on my way."

"She's beyond in the kitchen-garden picking gooseberries," Emily informed him. "When you give her the letter, you can have strawberries and cream if you want some."

"Thank you," Jonathan inclined his head civilly in acknowledgement of the gesture.

"We're under the big cedar," Miss Julie indicated a giant evergreen a little way from the house. "We'll have a nice chat," Miss Emily added. Jonathan took this to mean that the chat was to be the price of the strawberries. Chat was not the word he would apply to the string of questions the sisters would have stored up since his last visit. The odd thing was that he rarely answered truthfully and, despite the fact that they knew this, they were still willing to pose the questions. Jonathan guessed that they were entertained in some small way by what he told them and that possibly they were able to sift a few grains of truth from the great number of whoppers with which he presented them. He had no compunction about lying. Most of the questions were so outrageous that they deserved no better. Sometimes, he suspected that they were testing the limits of his imaginative powers. With him, it was a game. He was of the belief that it was the same with the sisters.

At first, he could see no trace of Jenny Stevens in the ancient, walled kitchen-garden. It was a grossly overgrown place with every plant in dire need of pruning. The place was jittery with songbirds. They started from every bush and tree as he followed the old stone path to the glass-house.

It was here he encountered Jenny Stevens. She was not alone. Jonathan recognized Bill Lunty. Lunty was the farm manager. He was a dark-haired, lusty fellow with stunningly white teeth which he revealed by means of a wide, ingratiating smile at every possible opportunity. He had his arms around Jenny Stevens who was making half-hearted attempts to resist him. He kissed her fiercely but she succeeded in pushing his head away. It was a type of kiss that Jonathan had not seen before. It was certainly not the kind of kiss he had so often seen his father give his mother, the sort of kiss everybody in the household might join in.

"You stop at once," Jenny was saying but beyond this she did not remonstrate further. Jonathan was surprised. She could have easily broken away if she had wanted to. Bill Lunty kissed her again, this time fully on the lips and afterwards on the face and neck. He drew her firmly against him. She offered no resistance whatsoever. Jonathan spoke from the shade of a dropping apple tree.

"Excuse me," he said. Bill Lunty released the girl at once. When Jenny saw who it was, she slapped the manager's face.

"You have a cheek," she said with a feigned anger. Lunty advanced on Jonathan and lifted him by both ears till their faces were level.

"What do you think you're doing?" he demanded angrily.

"Nothing," Jonathan replied as best he could from his position above the ground. His ears were beginning to hurt.

"Put him down at once," Jenny called.

"Why should I?" Lunty retorted savagely.

"Because," Jenny spoke with a trace of mockery, "his

father happens to be Ned Hindley." It had the desired effect. Jonathan was released.

"What do you mean?" Lunty shouted, "sneaking up on people without warning. Suppose I were to tell your father?" Jonathan, thankful to be on the ground, decided against answering lest he inadvertently say something which might further provoke Lunty.

"Did you come to see me about something, Jonathan?" Jenny asked politely. Jonathan tendered the letter. Jenny ripped it open at once and avidly read the solitary, crumpled sheet. Jonathan silently mouthed the message word for word in concert with her. He waited eagerly for her reaction.

"Tell that orphanage boy not to dare write to me again," she spoke shrilly. It was a glorious opportunity for comparing her legitimate background with one which seemed, in her eyes, to be less favorable. She looked the very personification of righteous indignation, her extraordinarily pretty face flushed disdainfully, her stance proud and haughty.

"Let's have a look," Lunty snatched the sheet from her hand and read it out loud. If his aim was to impress Jenny Stevens, he was successful. She burst out laughing as he perfectly mimicked the reticent Paddy Pine.

"Could I have the letter back, please?" Jonathan asked meekly.

"It's mine," Jenny replied perkily. "I'll keep it as a curio." Jonathan said nothing. Slowly, he turned and picked his way along the path. He ran quickly past the house to the amazement of the Misses Carter who awaited him under the big cedar.

"What do you suppose?" Miss Emily asked. There was no mistaking the disappointment in her voice.

"Boys," Miss Julie replied, "just boys. You can never tell with boys."

Paddy Pine listened for the third time to Jonathan's account of his visit to the Carters. Jonathan had not told of seeing the kissing session. Things were bad enough without including that. Neither did he reveal that Lunty had read the letter.

"You're sure that was her excuse?" Paddy pressed him. "That was exactly what she said," Jonathan lied, "tell him he's too young."

"Nothing more? Nothing more?" In time the whole household came to know of the letter. For Jenny Stevens, it was something of a romantic triumph. She showed it to less fortunate serving girls of her acquaintance. Word spread. It was an embarrassing period for Paddy Pine. He solved his problem by not going out at night. A month passed and the affair was forgotten.

Paddy's obsession with Jenny persisted. Neither Ned nor Hilary Hindley took it too seriously.

"We all must go through these phases," Ned submitted.

"It's not calf love," Hilary reminded him. "It's something more. It's rather sad for Paddy that it's so one-sided. Personally, I don't like the girl."

"You'll have to admit she's very pretty."

"I agree on that score but I do not see her as an ideal partner for Paddy."

"All she has to do is lift her little finger. He'll follow."

"That's what worries me," Hilary Hindley mused.

On his way from school, Jonathan called each afternoon to the village post office where he would collect the newspaper. If he had pocket money, he would indulge in an ice cream or a bar of chocolate. Generally, he would spend a quarter hour browsing through comics and magazines. The assistant was a red-haired girl named Nora Devane. Jonathan thought highly of her, so highly he kept her at the back of his mind as a prospective girlfriend for Paddy. She never objected when he thoroughly read a new comic which he might not be able to afford. She was only seventeen. He found her easy and pleasant to converse with. In addition, she had bright blue eyes and a pleasant smile.

Not long after his visit to the old house, he resolved to have a word with Nora. Instinctively, he knew that she would be a different proposition to Jenny Stevens. At least she would take him seriously. Of this he was convinced.

About a fortnight before Christmas, while he was rummaging through the comic stand, he succeeded in catching her eye. She came outside the counter as soon as she could.

"What is it, Jonathan?" she asked.

"Will you go with Paddy Pine?"

"Why doesn't he come and ask me himself?"

"Because he's shy," Jonathan told her.

"He's a nice boy," she said half to herself. Then to Jonathan, "I'll have to see. I just can't make up my mind all at once and anyway my mother likes me to tell her about dates. I'll let you know tomorrow."

Faithfully, after school, Jonathan called at the post office.

"The answer is yes," Nora whispered when she found it convenient to do so, "but he'll have to ask me himself."

That night, before they fell asleep, Jonathan paid a visit to Paddy's room. He sat on a small stool near the window and looked out into the river.

"It's high tonight," he said. Paddy lay on his bed fully awake, looking at the ceiling.

"You didn't see her lately?" he asked.

"Only in the distance," Jonathan answered.

"How can she be so cruel?" Paddy suddenly leaped from the bed and joined Jonathan at the window.

"All night I listen to the river and think of her," he said. "I think of little else. I try to drive her from my thoughts and think of other things but her face comes back from nowhere and I see her smile and laugh. I dream of her too. She runs along the river bank by the sallies and I follow."

"I met somebody today who was asking for you," Jonathan lied.

"Oh?" was all Paddy said.

"Yes," Jonathan seized his opportunity, "she'd like to go with you sometime."

"Who are you speaking about?"

"You know Nora Devane, the girl with the red hair who works in the post office."

"I know her. Why wouldn't I? Don't I see her every

Sunday when we call for the papers."

"She's a nice girl," Jonathan said, "I mean a really nice girl."

"I'm sure she is," Paddy sighed. He returned to the bed and drew the clothes over his head. Jonathan sat by the window, watching the moonlight play where the water was broken. Suddenly he felt lonely. The moon submitted herself to the shrouding clouds and a giant shadow came down the river. He rose from the chair and addressed himself to the form in the bed.

"Will you consider her?" he asked hopefully.

Paddy Pine's head emerged from beneath the bedclothes.

"Consider who?" he asked absently. Jonathan knew that further conversation would be a waste of time. For the next few days, he entrusted the collection of the newspaper to the twins. He decided he could not very well face Nora Devane under the circumstances. However, as Christmas drew near, he was forced to confront her. There were cards to be posted and gifts to be bought.

"He never called," was the first thing Nora said when he entered the shop.

"I told you he was shy," Jonathan returned.

"Well," she pouted, "if he's going to be that shy, where's the point?"

"Don't worry," Jonathan assured her, "he'll come round to it."

"Saint Stephen's night is only a week away," she reminded him.

Jonathan was well aware that the Saint Stephen's night dance was the most important one of the year. It was the accepted time for introducing new faces. There was also the fact that the youth of the district looked forward to it with an eagerness they did not reserve for other occasions. This might well be due to their being cooped up over the Christmas or it could be that it was the finale of the year's festivities. New Year's eve was less than a week later. Whatever it was, nothing less than a calamity could keep the young people home on that night.

"Do you think it's likely he'll be in to see me before Christmas?" Nora asked as soon as the shop was empty of customers.

"Most likely," Jonathan said.

"But how can I be sure?"

"You can be sure," Jonathan said it emphatically while he prayed that a customer would cross the threshold and spare him from further interrogation.

"I'll have to be going now," he told her, "I'm late as it is."

"Jonathan Hindley," she called after him, "are you sure you're not having me on?"

Jonathan ran quickly down the little street and turned into a laneway pretending he hadn't heard. He dawdled on the way home. Sooner or later he would have to take the bull by the horns and tell the truth to Nora. It might not be too bad if he didn't like her, but the fact remained that she was the only person in the village who consistently showed him kindness.

At the entrance to the Carter demesne which he passed each afternoon on his way home, he stopped to kick the carpeting of decaying leaves into a central mound.

So industrious was his assault that he failed to notice the figure in the rhododendrons immediately at his back. It was growing dusk at the time.

"Psst," came the whispered summons from the mouth of the figure in question but this he dismissed as the utterance of some insect or animal in the undergrowth.

"Hey! You!" a girl's voice called impatiently. Jonathan was taken completely by surprise. He turned quickly as a girl with a headscarf tightly bound round her head appeared from the deepening dusk. Jonathan failed to identify her at first.

"Who ... who's there?" he asked nervously. Cautiously, he retreated a step. There had been talk some years previously of an apparition at this very entrance.

"Don't run away, please," the girl said. "It's me, Jenny Stevens."

"What is it you want?" Jonathan was still nervous.

"I've been waiting for you," she said. "I have to speak to you."

"About what?"

"The Pine boy. Is he still interested, do you think?"

"Yes," Jonathan replied.

"You're sure?"

"Yes," he told her, "I'm sure."

"I want you to give him a message. It's especially for him. Nobody else must know." Jonathan nodded. He took advantage of her nearness to examine her face. She was very pretty but there were dark lines under her eyes and her cheeks were indrawn. All in all, there was a gauntness about her face which gave it a frightened look.

"Nobody knows I'm here," she said desperately. "I've been waiting for nearly an hour. Are you always as late as this?"

Jonathan shook his head. There was an unexpected breathlessness abut her that he associated with older women.

"Are you sick?" he asked.

"No. No," she replied at once. "I never felt better in my life. It's the cold. I've been standing here so long that it's got inside me. Why do you look at me like that?"

"I'm sorry," he said awkwardly, "you've changed somehow."

"Am I less pretty?" she asked the question confidently.

"It's not that," he said with difficulty.

"I know. I know," she said quickly. "I've lost weight. That's what it is. Now listen carefully, Jonathan. You tell Paddy Pine that I'm leaving for England in the morning. Tell him to meet me here. The half eight bus stops right at this gate week mornings. I'll be waiting. You'll tell him that?"

"Yes," Jonathan said. She gave him the message over and over and asked him to say it for her. He had to repeat himself again and again until she was assured that he had it correctly by heart.

"No matter what," she insisted, "nobody must know.

JONATHAN

197

I wouldn't like if anybody did and you know he wouldn't like it. Give me your oath that you'll tell nobody but him."

"I can't give my oath," Jonathan sounded adamant about it. "That's a mortal sin."

"Your word of honor then?"

"Alright," he said. "I give my word of honor."

"You're a good boy," she told him. "Now hurry home and tell him. There will be things he must do." Squeezing his arm, she hurried up the avenue. He stood for a while, deep in thought, after she had gone. Slowly he made the sign of the cross and looked upwards.

"God," he said, "you heard me whisper that I was crossing out the promise of my word the moment I gave it. This is to make sure you heard."

Darkness had fallen by the time he entered the brightly-lit kitchen of his home.

"What in God's name kept you, Jonathan?" Hilary Hindley asked. "Have you been fighting again?"

Jonathan shook his head. Hilary shook hers.

"Call your father and Paddy like a good boy. Supper's ready."

After supper, the rain fell. It drummed on the corrugated roofs of the outhouses. Everywhere, rivulets were forming and running with increasing volume to the river. It was a steady, heavy rain that lasted well into the morning. Jonathan was out of bed by eight o'clock. At half past, he hid himself close by a stand of roadside spruce about fifty yards from the Carter gate. There was no sign of the girl. He waited patiently until he heard the faint rumble of the approaching bus. As it neared the gate, the gears changed hoarsely and the outsize vehicle drew to a squealing halt.

Suddenly, Jenny Stevens appeared. Her head was covered with a headscarf as before and she carried a large suitcase in her hand. Her long, blue gabardine coat hung unbuttoned by her sides. Vainly, she looked up and down the road. Desperately, she signaled to the driver for a moment or two of grace. He waited a full minute. Then he blew on the hooter. With a dark look on her face, she boarded the bus.

Paddy Pine lay on the bed. He had spent a melancholy day. At the creamery he learned of Jenny's departure the day before. Everybody seemed to know she had left for England. No particular person had informed him. He had overheard.

Quietly, Jonathan entered the room. He sat on the stool by the window and looked out.

"The water's falling," he said. "I can tell by the sound." When Paddy failed to comment, Jonathan tried a new tack.

"Several have asked Nora Devane to the dance on Saint Stephen's night. She doesn't know what to do. What will I say to her?"

Paddy sat up on the bed.

"I don't know," he said.

"I think you should come and ask her tomorrow before it's too late."

"But I hardly know her."

"I think it's a terrible thing," Jonathan announced

righteously, "that a girl as good-looking as Nora Devane should be left hanging there just because you won't ask her. It's you she wants. She said so. She must have told me ten times. She really likes you."

"But how can she like me so much when I only know her to see her?"

"I don't know," Jonathan replied. "Just imagine that she likes you as much as you liked Jenny Stevens and you'll know what it's like for her."

A thoughtful look settled on Paddy's face. He sat on the side of the bed. Jonathan guessed that he was puzzling out the implications of what he had just said. After a while, Paddy spoke.

"I know what you mean," he said.

"I'll see you in the village then, tomorrow after school. She'll be delighted."

"You really think so?" There was a look of uncertainty on Paddy's face.

"I know so," Jonathan concluded as he left the room hurriedly in case Paddy started to have misgivings.

Downstairs, Ned and Hilary Hindley sat by the fire. Each was preoccupied, Ned with the day's paper and Hilary with a pullover which was to be part of Jonathan's Christmas box. Out of the blue, Hilary spoke.

"I'm worried about Jonathan," she said. Ned Hindley put the paper to one side.

"What's he been up to?" he asked.

"I don't know," she said. "He was two hours coming from school today and most of the time he acts as though his mind was elsewhere. You think he's a bright boy?" Ned Hindley laughed.

"I wouldn't worry about Master Jonathan," he said. "There's more to him than meets the eye." Reassured, Hilary resumed her knitting.

"Jenny Stevens is gone to England since yesterday," Ned informed her.

"I'm not surprised," Hilary sighed.

"She looked a bit peakish lately. You think there's something wrong?"

"I'm certain of it," Hilary answered, "and, from the looks of her, it's been wrong with a while."

The Reek

The bog was a mixture of browns and grays, gray where the sun had bleached the exposed turf banks and the misshapen reeks of yesteryear which stood along the margin of the roadway. In the moonlight, the gray turned to silver but the brown remained somber even when stars danced and the heavens seemed on fire. When the weather was fine, the bog was my playground. Every goat-path, bog-hole and goose-nest was as familiar to me as the lanes and streets of the nearby town where I lived. I knew the titles of the turf banks and the names of the reek owners. I knew the sod depth of every bank and the quagmires where asses and ponies sank to their haunches. This was because I spent most of the summer days with two ancient relatives who lived in a tiny thatched house on the edge of the bog. They were brothers. Their names were Mr. Chamberlain and Sir Stafford Cripps. These, of course, were not their real names. Rather were they sobriquets invented by the locals on account of the resemblance the pair bore to the British politicians Neville Chamberlain and Stafford Cripps. The Second World War was well under way when I discovered the bog and there was an abundance of Rommells, Montys and McArthurs so christened because of forecasts they might have made regarding the outcome of the war or because of certain characteristics relating to the famous generals.

Mr. Chamberlain was the older of the two brothers. He was lean as a whippet, bald as a coot and reticent to the point of muteness. Sir Stafford, on the other hand, was as talkative as he was outgoing. Both were on the old age pension. It was Sir Stafford who tackled the ass and went to town on Fridays to cash the pension vouchers. Mr. Chamberlain would not demean himself with such mundane matters and only went to town on Sundays to attend Mass. The pair got on famously. Sometimes there were disagreements but these were short-lived. I remember one such. It was early September. The turf was harvested and new reeks were beginning to appear daily on the roadway. The brothers had earlier cut, stooked and re-stooked two sleans of turf and this stood now in donkey stoolins in the bog on the heather-covered turf bank which had supplied them with turf for generations. It would have to be transported from the bank to the roadway where it would be built into a reek.

Mid-August to mid-September was the recognized time for drawing out. The passages to the turf banks were dry and firm but later they might be rendered impassable by heavy rains. When this happened, the turf remained in the bog until the late spring of the following year and the owners had to make do with the remains of old reeks and occasional sacks laboriously drawn on their backs from the stranded stoolins.

"It's time," Mr. Chamberlain announced as we sat on the low wall which fronted the house.

"And I say it's not time," Sir Stafford countered.

"And why so do you say that?" Mr. Chamberlain asked, "when I say otherwise."

"I say that," said Sir Stafford, "because the man on Hanafin's wireless made a forecast of rain."

"And what do he know?" Mr. Chamberlain asked derisively, "that couldn't tell one end of this bog from the other, no more nor the ass."

"He knows plenty," Sir Stafford persisted.

"There will be no rain tomorrow," Mr. Chamberlain spoke with finality. "The wind is from the right point and there's heating in it and if there's heating in it then by all the laws the sun will be along after the wind."

To give confirmation to his belief, he raised his head

and turned his thin, sensitive nose into the wind. I did likewise. The sea was less than five miles distant as the crow flies and sometimes there was a tang of salt in the air. Other times, especially after high tides, there would be a strong fragrance of sea wrack. Often there was the unmistakable odor of decay but it was always possible for a man of experience and judgment to smell out any rain that might be likely to move inland in the course of time.

"There's no rain in that, no rain at all." So saying, Mr. Chamberlain rose unsteadily from his seat and sauntered down the roadway towards the passage which led to the turf bank. He had aged more during this summer than he had in all the years since I knew him. He still walked erectly if somewhat irresolutely. There were hints of debilitation in all his steps.

"There's a stagger to him," Stafford Cripps whispered. I knew what this meant. A stagger was taken to mean that a man was nearing his end, maybe not immediately nor for a considerable time. It was a telling factor, however, from which there was no reprieve.

Later that evening, I was invited to participate in the drawing out. I was to be in charge of transport. Cripps was to be posted on the turf bank where he would assist in filling the ass rails. Mr. Chamberlain was designated reek maker. He had somewhat of a reputation in this field and it would have been unthinkable to have invested him with a less onerous task.

The following day broke bright and clear. There was little or no wind but the air was crisp and cool. The sky was free of cloud and it looked as if the day would be a fine one. Mr. Chamberlain had been correct in his forecast for, as the morning wore on and the sun climbed higher in the sky, it grew distinctly warmer. Each time I heeled the ass cart and emptied a fresh load, Mr. Chamberlain nodded his appreciation but made no attempt to start building the reek. He merely indicated where he wanted the cart heeled. He knew exactly what he was doing of course. Earlier, he had counted the donkey stoolins and made an estimate of the space he would need to contain the entire harvest. He measured his ground with even paces and then with boot lengths for exactitude until a rectangular base was plotted. I had seen him make reeks before. There was no more meticulous builder in the bog. This time, he seemed to be more fastidious than ever. He weighed the turf sods with greater care and, occasionally, he placed a particularly large and well-shaped brick to one side. These would be used later in the clamping.

All morning we worked and, as we did, the September sun ascended the cloudless heavens. For every step it took upwards, the reek took another. At noon, we broke for food. This had been painstakingly prepared by the brothers. Mr. Chamberlain had lighted a fire during one of my journeys to the turf bank. Atop it sat a kettle of boiling water, a continuous jet of steam shooting from its shapely spout. Wrapped in white muslin was a sizable wedge of boiled bacon and, in another cloth, was a pound or so of fresh cheese. There was also a loaf of homemade bread and a solid slab of butter. As soon as the tea was drawn, we set about eating. In between mouthfuls, Sir Stafford would make a pronouncement.

"There is no sauce like bog air."

I was too preoccupied to comment one way or the other.

"Plain food is the best food," from Sir Stafford again. It went on like this until we had eaten and drunk our fill. Then we sat back and relaxed awhile. This was the best part of the day. Other men who were occupied as we were came to join us in order to debate the course of the war. Mingled scents of heather and woodbine imposed themselves fleetingly over the pedestrian odors of the roadway. There was time to savor the sunlit beauty of the bogland while the men spoke on and on of important happenings. Endlessly, larks rose carolling from hidden haunts in the heather. The air was clear as far as the eye could see. The little haze there was had long since been burned up by the hot sun. The talk now dwelt on the subject of townspeople.

"I have seen them," Sir Stafford was saying, "and they racking their hair before stooking the turf. I have seen them and they wearing low shoes only fit for dancing and they trying to operate a slean."

Here Mr. Chamberlain made one of his very rare contributions to the proceedings.

"I seen the first of the turf-cutting townies at the start of the war," he said. "They came in droves when the coal got scarce. I seen strange things but I never before seen the likes of these men. They had bread with meat in the middle of it. You could only see the edge of the meat. The rest was covered by bread above and below. There is no way you could inveigle me to eat meat I couldn't see."

"It must be sandwiches you're talking about," Sir Stafford put in.

"The very thing. The very thing indeed. That was the name given to them."

The talk wore on. It was of times gone by when men worked for coppers and promises and often turned over in their beds at night in an effort to dispel the hollow growling of hunger in empty stomachs. They spoke of spailpíns and laborers who worked from dawn till dark and who had nothing at all to show for their labors in the end, nothing but stooped backs and strained limbs. They spoke of the immeasurable value of booklearning as the one true avenue of escape from drudgery and expressed regrets for the way they had neglected their books in favor of youthful dalliance.

"A schoolmaster now," someone said, "he earns a sovereign a day and he don't bend his back."

"No wonder they're cracked," Sir Stafford commented, "money like that would go to any man's head."

Elsewhere, the fate of the world was being decided. Far away in Cairo, Churchill and Roosevelt were meeting with Chiang Kai Shek and, in southern Italy, fierce battles were raging as the Allies endeavored to advance northwards. We sat drowsily in the lee of the reek grateful for the warm sunshine. The conversation started to flag with the realization that the time had come to resume work. Later, there would be another break for what was known as "the evening tay." This consisted of a panny of tea and a slice or two of bread and butter. It was generally a hurried affair at which no time was wasted. There was still some talk but the conversation had lost much of its sparkle. I was despatched in search of the donkey. He had not ventured far. There was an abundance of good grass and wild clover at hand on the margins of the roadway. He allowed himself to be recaptured without resistance as though he knew instinctively that the day was far from being down and there was no point in prolonging his legal recess. I tackled him to the cart without difficulty and, in a short while, we were working as a unit once more. The pace had quickened as if by agreement although not a word passed between us. There was an urgency to the work now. The pressure would have to be maintained if we were to finish by evening. After "the evening tay" the old men seemed to grow tired. So did I but it would never do to give the impression that one was unable to pull one's weight. The pace was relentless now but no quarter was asked or given. It would not be too long before the last of the stoolins was on the roadway. It was heartening to see the decrease in their number.

The reek was really taking shape now, assuming that peculiar symmetry with which only a countryman could invest it. There was something here above and beyond blueprints and drawing boards. There was an instinctive insight into the secret shape of the land itself and into this was fitted unobstructively the dark contours of the reek. Instead of standing out, it fitted in like a patch into a quilt.

I noticed too that it did not run in a precise parallel line with the roadway. Its strongest shoulder, better buttressed than the others, stood in the face of the prevailing south-westerly wind. Immense knowledge about the peculiar tantrums and exact route of this wind was essential if the reek was to survive the vicissitudes of winter and any reek, no matter how large, was, after all, only as strong as its weakest point. From time to time, Mr. Chamberlain would walk slowly round its base searching for inadequacies. Often too, he would remove himself from the immediate vicinity of the reek and survey it with a critical eye from a distance. He observed it from every angle and from every posture. One moment, he would be standing on the tips of his toes and, the next, he would be lying prone. He inspected it from his haunches and he went so far as to kneel in the center of the roadway to determine if the upward inclination was gradual enough. Nothing was left to chance. Never before had he been so finical. As the evening wore on, he grew somewhat irritable but this passed when the reek reached a certain stage in its development.

Sod by sod, foot by foot, it rose to its smoothly taper-ing roof until the last ass-load had been deposited on the roadway. All that was left on the turf bank was a carpet of dust and tiny cadhrawns. Sir Stafford and I untackled the ass. At once he rolled over and over on the dusty roadway, braying ecstatically. When he had rolled his fill he flicked his hind legs defiantly and cantered down a narrow cause-way where a green patch of good grass advertized itself.

The reek was finished except for a few final touches. The clamping was impeccable. Hardly the width of a grass blade divided sod from sod. Sir Stafford now took a turn around it, pausing to inspect a particularly impressive piece of cornering. With the aid of the ass-cart, Mr. Chamberlain mounted the reek and sat astride its roof. I stood by with a gabhail of assorted sods. Occasionally, there would be a surgical extension of his hand and I would tender a sod. He might or might not accept it, favoring another of different size or shape. It seemed to me that he was overdoing it. Now, with hindsight, I know that he was merely a thorough and conscientious craftsman who selected sods and parts of sods the way a poet might select words or phrases essential to the immaculate completion of the work in hand.

Also, the finished work would be submitted for critical analysis although it would be true to say that the most just and impartial critics of all would be the north-easterly and south-westerly winds. These were the lads who wouldn't be long pinpointing flaws. The accredited critics came that very evening. These were accomplished reekers themselves. All the reviews were favorable with the exception of the usual carper or two whose own reeks could never stand up to penetrating criticism.

"That won't be knocked aisy," one white-haired onlooker essayed.

"That," said Sir Stafford Cripps pointedly, "won't be knocked at all."

The days passed. Autumn went its way in a flurry of

russets and winter appeared, unexpected as always, but predictably harsh and cold with mighty storms that ranted and raged across the countryside. The reek was not found wanting under the onslaught. It was its maker who was to prove suspect. In January, he contracted a heavy cold and, because he would accept advice from nobody and stay indoors like a sensible fellow, he developed pneumonia and had to be removed to hospital. His condition weakened and, one spring morning, when the last of the wild geese were winging their way northward, he died in his sleep. Shortly after Mr. Chamberlain's demise, Sir Stafford was smitten by influenza but the neighbors, fearful lest he should be swept away like his brother, maintained a constant vigil and by the middle of March he was on his feet once more, hale and hearty. The reek stood for the remainder of that year without interference. Sir Stafford made do with old turf which lay in a shed at the rear of the cottage. When the season for turf-cutting was under way, he hired three young men from the locality to cut a brace of sleans. The reek he left untouched. His decision was not questioned. Artistically, it was the best designed and most shapely fabrication of its kind to have been constructed on the roadway for generations. During its third year, there was considerable shrinkage but, such was the character of the design in the original structure, there was still no unevenness nor was there the slightest evidence of depression from end to end. Now denuded of its original brown by the years of wind and rain, its bleached exterior gave the impression that it had been frosted all over. On clear nights, under an unshrouded moon, it seemed as if it were a great rampart of silver.

Then, of a gusty March evening, a large band of traveling people appeared at the entrance to the bog. They liked what they saw. They were impressed by the green of the cutaway and, if it was a faded green itself, the ponies, horses and asses of which the train was mainly comprised were anything but choosy. Down the road they came in three multicolored, horse-drawn caravans, flanked and trailed by a motley assortment of the most heterogeneous mongrels imaginable. It was a swift-moving but silent caravan. Its occupants, animal and human, were feeling their way. The faces of the menfolk who led the caravan horses were blue with cold. Their noses ran freely. From time to time, they would press a finger against one side and expel the rheumy contents of the free nostril with snorts and grunts. As they approached the reek, a flock of children suddenly appeared from the interior of the caravans and started to play games on the roadway, contriving, at the same time, to stay in front of the three caravans. When all had passed, it was plain to be seen that the reek would never be the same again. There were gaping black holes and cavities along the side nearest to the roadway. Sir Stafford had never taken his eyes from the passing train. Still he had been caught napping by the children's diversions. He knew from long experience that a search of the caravans would reveal nothing. The stolen turf would be instantly and secretively jettisoned at the first sign of danger. Sir Stafford was furious. The reek was now scarred and ulcerous and prey to rain and storm. It would collapse completely in a matter of weeks, particularly since it was now certain that further inroads would be made into its already gutted side.

Night came. The fires of the travelers burned brightly in the deep of the bog. Sir Stafford sensed that they would stay awhile, in all probability till the end of April. The reek would stand no chance.

He had looked upon it as a monument to the late Mr. Chamberlain. He foresaw a time when it would have naturally and gracefully disintegrated just like its maker but he had never allowed for the intolerable rape of that afternoon. He knew exactly what must be done. In the cottage hearth, he built a great fire of heavy black sods. When the coals glowed red, he transferred them to a tin bucket and made straight for the reek. The wind was from the east but it was dry and crisp. He selected a favorable spot and withdrew several sods from the base. These he replaced with the glowing coals. For the freshening breeze, it was a labor of love to achieve the rest.

Death Be Not Proud

The land meant everything to Mick Henderson. The cardinal rule of his long life was its preservation. Envious neighbors whose own land had become run down through neglect and laziness would have outsiders believe that he loved the land more than he loved his wife and certainly more than he loved his family. This was not so. He had been fond of his wife when he married. He had remained fond of her through storm and calm over the years and even now, when the physical aspect of his marriage was becoming something of a memory, he treasured her companionship in a way that only long attachment can foster.

He would have been hard put to explain his obsession with the land. His wife understood fully and there were others like himself in the valley who felt as he did. These would be silent, tight-lipped men, not without humor and not given to vindicating or modifying what would seem to be an extraordinary preoccupation with the soil.

At seventy, Mick Henderson found himself in a quandary. Labor was becoming impossible to come by. Factories were shooting up like thistles in the nearby towns and cities. Whatever workforce was available in the area was almost completely absorbed. Even his regular workman had deserted him for lucrative shift work and a five-day week. The latter was something of a joke amongst the farming community. All the holdings supported herds of milch cows and during the heavy milking periods these needed constant attention.

Once, when endeavoring to hire a workman, Mick was asked if he would settle for a five-day week. "You can have a one-day week in the winter," Mick had told him, "but until such time as we have a five-day cow there will be no five-day week."

He had gone so far as to offer free Sundays during the peak periods and occasional days off for special events but there was no competing with the attractions of the factories. He cut down his herd to a manageable size although he was still heavily in debt from having put three sons and two daughters through boarding schools and colleges.

There was another son, Mikey, named after himself, a black sheep of sorts, who disappeared one morning when he was barely sixteen after a vicious row regarding his attitude towards further schooling. That was nearly ten years before. Mick Henderson knew his son's address in England, knew he was doing well as a chargehand in a Coventry factory, knew enough in fact to make Mikey feel downright uncomfortable if he ever suspected such paternal interest.

The others had no feeling for the land, no concern about it. On his seventieth birthday, he had betaken himself to the city to consult with his eldest son, Maurice, who was a solicitor there. After listening carefully for over half an hour, Maurice submitted his opinion.

"Your safest and your easiest course," he said dispassionately, "is to sell out and live here in Dublin or, if city life has no appeal for you, there is nothing to prevent you from buying a comfortable house in the country. The money you would make from the sale would clear your debts and leave you with more than sufficient to ensure a comfortable life for mother and yourself until the end of your days."

His second son, Eddie, was a dentist. Married with two children, he operated from a small surgery attached to his home in the suburbs. Late as it was when Tom called, he found Eddie up to his eyes in work. Very late that night they sat round the sitting-room fire and talked about the land. It was impossible not to like Eddie and his wife but they had little to offer by way of a solution. They also felt that selling the land would be the best way out.

It was the third son, Martin, a civil servant, who supplied the obvious answer. Mick had a job finding his house in the sprawling, estate-cluttered northside of the metropolis. Snugly seated in the back seat of a taxi he passed row after row of newly-erected, two-storied houses. After numerous enquiries they eventually discovered the estate. Another search and they located the house. It stood amid hundreds of others which looked exactly alike.

"How in the name of God does anyone live here?" he had asked undiplomatically when Martin and his wife met him at the door.

"You get used to it," Martin said, enjoying his father's perplexity.

In spite of his first impression he was pleasantly surprised by the interior of the house. It had a heartening spaciousness in contrast to what he had expected.

"You have a fine home, Martin," he announced by way of conciliation.

"It's only a few hundred yards from the school," Martin's wife said, "and that's what really matters."

After the usual preliminaries, Mick settled down to the business of outlining his problems. Martin and his wife listened sympathetically while he explained about the new factories and the scarcity of labor.

"The last thing I want to do is sell it," he finished.

"The logical thing, as far as I can see, is to bring Mikey back from Coventry," Martin suggested.

"Will he want to come back?" Mick asked.

"I have no doubt that he will," Martin assured him.

Mick Henderson considered this for some time. It was a thought that had always been at the back of his head. All he needed was someone, other than himself, to suggest it. He was aware that Martin and Mikey were as close as brothers could be despite the distance that separated them. In age, there was hardly a year between them. It was to be expected, therefore, that Martin would put forward a strong case for the youngest brother. Mick Henderson decided that he would find out how forceful Martin's advocacy might be.

"That's all very fine," he said disinterestedly, "but has he the feel for the land?"

"Why wouldn't he?" Martin hastened to reply, "he's your son, isn't he?"

"You're my son and you have no feel for it. Neither has Maurice or Eddie."

"Look," Martin pleaded, "Mikey is different. He's only good with his hands. He was a hopeless scholar. If you had kept him at home when he kicked off the traces that first time he'd know it all now and you wouldn't be worrying about labor."

"'Tis easy be wise after the event," Mick Henderson said. He suspected that Mikey might have the true feeling for the land but there was no way he could be certain. He resolved to probe further.

"What guarantee have I that he won't flog the farm as soon as I pass on?" he asked.

"That's a chance you'll have to take but let me tell you this. Mikey is hardly likely to flog it when it's going to be his livelihood. You know as well as I that he knew how to handle livestock. That time before he ran away, he had no objection to working on the farm. What he objected to was school."

"Agreed," Mick Henderson returned, "but there's many a young lad will volunteer for anything to escape school."

"I happen to know," Martin's tone was really serious now, "that if he doesn't come home this year he won't come home at all."

"Did he say this?"

"Yes."

"Then I suppose I had better contact him. What if he says no?"

"That's one thing he won't say," Martin assured him. After this conversation, Mick Henderson had no doubt in his mind that Martin and Mikey had discussed his position in depth. On his way home by train, he had ample time to think. His one fear was that the land might be sold after his death but this would happen anyway if Mikey refused to come home. He remembered when the farm had been signed over to him by his own father. It had been a bright May morning close on forty years before. He had no idea what his father's business in the neighboring town might be when he instructed him to tackle the black mare to the family trap. By midday, he was the legal owner of the land. He had in no way pressurized his father although he had dropped hints that he was thinking of getting married. It was somewhat different in his case. The true feeling for the land was there. His father knew this, knew that the green pastures to which he had devoted the best years of his life would be safe for another generation. It was so important that Mikey have this feeling for the acres which would shortly be under his care. Mick Henderson knew everything there was to be known about the land. Over the years, he had discovered its idiosyncrasies and failings and learned painstakingly how to turn deficiencies into advantages. The land had its own unique characteristics, its own vague, imperceptible contours, its inexplicable portions of soft and hard, wet and dry, barren and lush.

On the surface, the fields were like any other in the district but he knew better. His father had been a source of constant help as he endeavored to discover the true lie of the land. Now that he knew all there was to be known, it was high time the knowledge was passed on. He would announce his decision to his wife Julia as soon as he got home. She would be pleased. He was aware that she secretly pined after her youngest son although, like all mothers, she became somewhat resigned to his absence as time went by.

The proper thing for me to do, Mick thought, is to impress upon him, without seeming to do so, the value of well-treated land. I will show him that, while human life is to be valued more than anything else, that which sustains it should be valued no less. I will pass over and my wife will pass over but the land will remain. We are only passing through, mere tenants at best. The land will be there forever to nurture my seed and the seed of my seed. Somehow he would try to get these feelings through to Mikey. If the genuine consciousness was there, this would be no problem. If Mikey did not fully respond, all would not be lost. At least he would not sell and the land would be saved. If one generation failed to throw up a man with love for the land the next generation was sure to compensate. Who could tell but he might live to see a grandson blessed with the appropriate and peculiar disposition so difficult to define.

Mikey Henderson arrived home during the second week of spring. The roadside hedgebanks were bright with clusters of early primroses and along the sides of the avenue leading to the old farmhouse were healthy clumps of daffodils and irises in various stages of flower. It was a good time to come home. During the first months, he made many mistakes but Mick was not slow to notice that he never made the same mistake a second time. He was uncannily adept with all sorts of machinery. He understood cattle and, most important of all, he knew how to husband his strength. He fitted perfectly into the pattern of things.

Mick watched his progress with the keenest interest. Who knew but some evening he might see Mikey, with his hands on his hips, surveying the sheen of a freshly-ploughed tillage field or shading his eyes against a summer sun on the headland of a meadow ripe for cutting.

With the coming of summer, the new green grass, luscious and fleecy, returned to the fields. The hedgerows, no longer bare, hosted a thousand songbirds and the first of the long herbage took the naked look from the broad meadows.

The meadows would prove to be the chief of Mikey's

problems that first summer. It wasn't a particularly good year for growth. The new crops were light and late and, to crown the general misfortune of the farming community, there was no labor available when the outlook was favorable for harvesting. The weather too was unkind. To say the least, it was inconsistent. Fine days were few and far between and rarely succeeded each other. During this time came the worst calamity that could possibly befall. Julia Henderson took ill and had to be removed to hospital. All thoughts of harvesting had to be abandoned until she recovered.

It was two weeks before she was released. She had undergone a mild coronary. Her doctor warned that unless she cut down considerably in her everyday work there would be a recurrence. After her short stay in hospital she felt refreshed and the tiredness which had nagged her for so long seemed to have disappeared altogether. She herself declared that she felt twenty years younger and insisted in shouldering her full quota of chores. A young girl was found locally to help her. She agreed to stay until the schools reopened in September. Outwardly, at any rate, Julia Henderson seemed very much rejuvenated. She looked the picture of health and there was none of the breathlessness which she so often endured before her visit to hospital.

There was a general air of excitement all over the district when the weather changed for the better. Despite the fact that there was no immediate prospect of labor, Mick and Mikey Henderson decided to make an all-out assault on the uncut meadows. All day, they followed each other on two tractors. In their wake, the tall grass fell in long parallel swathes. Julia and the girl brought their meals to the meadow. There was no tarrying for small-talk afterwards. As soon as they had eaten, they mounted the cumbersome machines. The onslaught lasted until the first faint stars appeared in the late evening sky. The moment they finished, they headed straight for the local pub. It wasn't that they especially needed a drink. It was the only place where they were likely to recruit labor. They were partly successful. It was first necessary to invest in several rounds of drink and to exhibit an interest in the welfare of likely prospects that was tantamount to fawning. This, with the offer of almost double the normal wage, was responsible for the extraction of three promises. Both Mick and Mikey were well aware that the trio in question were not exactly the cream of the crop. They would be late and they would put no great strain on themselves but they were laborers and, if the weather held, the produce of the combined meadows might be saved at the end of three days.

For most of the first day, they turned and then tossed the freshly mown swathes. Late in the afternoon, they made it up into windrows in preparation for the following day's cocking. This completed, they broke off. That night, the Hendersons listened avidly to the weather forecast. Prospects were still good. Mick and Mikey rose with the dawn. First, the cows had to be milked. Then the milk had to be cooled and transported to the creamery. After that, it was straight to the meadow. Everything else was secondary. The laborers arrived at ten o'clock and then the business of cocking commenced. First, the crisp hay had to be gathered by the tractor-drawn, iron-toothed rake. Mikey attended to this particular function. He worked furiously, supplying the needs of the cock-makers who worked in pairs. When the supply exceeded demand, he would jump from the tractor and shoulder huge pikefuls of hay to the base of the developing cock. This was the hardest part of haymaking. One by one, slowly and painfully, the cocks went up until by the end of the second day half the entire crop was safe. The midday meal was brought to the meadow by Julia Henderson and the girl. On the third day, Julia came alone. The girl had not shown up. Enquiry revealed that she had been at a dance the night before and was unable to get out of bed. Julia was not unprepared. She arrived at the meadow shortly after noon, just as the sky was undergoing a murky suffusion to the south-west. If rain was to come, this would be the direction from which it would threaten. After the meal, one of the laborers announced that he was unable to continue because of a stomach ailment. Mick guessed that the pace was not to his liking. The same man had shown himself to be somewhat of a shirker from the beginning. Mikey had heard him derogatorily remarking to one of his colleagues that if he was to die he wouldn't like it to be for a farmer.

Despite her husband's protestations, Julia insisted in falling in by his side. They worked together, silently, at a corner of the meadow far removed from the other pair. Julia Henderson was the ideal farmer's wife. Always, she had been by her husband's side when the need was there. Of solid farming stock herself, she was aware of her obligations although these had often ranged from milking the entire herd to deputizing at weddings and funerals. This was the unwritten law when labor was not to be had.

Now and then, Mick would glance anxiously to the west and south where the ominous turgescence of massing clouds was slowly enveloping the otherwise clear sky. By his own reckoning, he estimated that there were three, maybe four good hours left. Given that much time, all the hay would undoubtedly be saved. He redoubled his own efforts and then, without warning of any kind, Julia Henderson heaved a massive, choking sigh. Mick stood helpless and appalled while she attempted to restrain with clutching fingers the terrible upheaval in her chest. Then, just as suddenly, her hands fell listlessly to her sides and she fell backwards noiselessly in a crumpled heap. Urgently, Mick Henderson bent and whispered an act of contrition into her ear. There was no disputing the fact that she was dead. He stretched her legs gently and folded her hands across her bosom.

Then he sat by her side awaiting the arrival of Mikey with the next rake of hay. The young man sensed something was wrong. He dismounted slowly from the tractor and read the news in his father's face. He knelt by his mother's side and kissed her on the lips and forehead. He smoothed back the hair from her face and lifted her head so that he could rest it on the pillow of hay. Then he rose and looked at the sky.

"Let's get on with it," he said. At first, Mick Henderson looked at him uncomprehendingly. Then the logic of it dawned on him.

"What about the two?" he asked, pointing to where the laborers were building a cock at the other end of the meadow.

"What they don't know won't trouble them," said Mikey, dismissing the question. Slowly his father rose. Already, Mikey was adding to the half-made cock. Instinctively, his father followed his example.

Before departing for another rake-up, Mikey laid a hand on his father's shoulder.

"She would understand," he said. "I don't have to tell you that. When the job is done we'll take her indoors. Then I'll go for a priest."

So saying, he mounted the machine and in a matter of seconds was again raking the ever-decreasing wind-rows. Mick Henderson cast a glance at his dead wife and then his eyes followed his youngest son. Beyond doubt, here was a man with a sound sense of priorities, a man with a true feel for the land.